CHRONICLES OF ESHA I

CROWNING
OF THE
SWORD

TABITHA DAY

ISBN 978-0-473-70915-0 (ePub)

ISBN 978-0-473-70914-3 (Paperback)

ISBN 978-0-473-70916-7 (Kindle)

Cover designed by GetCovers

Powered by Atticus

For you,
adventurer, dreamer, hero.

CHAPTER 1

T he front door crashed open and struck the wall before slamming shut again, the sound reverberating up through the floorboards.

In her bed, Ember froze, her breathing still deep and slow as if she were sleeping, but her body alert, every muscle, tendon, and sinew tense, ready.

There was always the dilemma of what to do when Bruno came home from a night out. Pretend to sleep and hope he would let her continue the charade, or get up and brace herself for whatever mood he was in. There were only those two choices, and whichever she chose depended on how brave or aggrieved she was feeling.

She could usually predict his temper by his tread on the stairs. Light and eager meant he'd had a win on the horses, or someone had flirted with him. Slow and heavy meant *watch out*. Sometimes there were no footsteps at all, and she'd find him flaked out on the couch in the lounge, stewed and snoring, all stale beer breath and sweat patches. That was always better.

Tonight, she couldn't tell what his tread meant. Still, she could deal with it, whatever *it* was going to be. It was going to be the last time, after all.

The bedroom door creaked open, and she took heart from that. At least he was giving the illusion of being conciliatory. He undressed, the mattress tilting under his weight. She waited for his meaty hand to crawl across the blankets like a fleshy spider to feast upon her, but he simply lay down. His breathing soon became as slow and even as hers, but she could tell something was off. Usually, Bruno's sleeping filled the room with snuffles and snorts, the churning of digestive acids, and the trumpeting of boozy farts that made the sheets reek. This morning however, he lay in silence.

Slowly, she turned her head on the pillow and cracked an eye.

He was staring straight at her.

The early morning light made his face look grey and drawn. The good looks that had first attracted her to him were long gone, hidden under red veined, bloated flesh and a layer of stubborn discontent.

"I knew you were awake." He sounded pleased with himself. "Can't fool me."

She made a show of yawning, made her voice slow and sleepy. "Hi, baby. Did you have a good night?"

"Too hot," he grumbled. "Hotter than custard."

Which didn't really make sense, but she wasn't about to argue. Temperatures *had* been soaring lately. Old Mrs Hughes from the school had fainted inside her parked car and would have died if two kids walking past hadn't seen her slumped over the wheel and dragged her out. Authorities had banned open fires for months now, although some had started spontaneously. There was that farm out west with the compost heap that had gone up, taking out three acres of dry grass before dying out at a creek bed. It was a miracle, the fire chief said on the tv news. Beside him, the farmer had a mixed look of shame and pride on his face—shame for the fire he'd caused, pride that it hadn't turned the entire town to ash.

Every day dawned a hard bright blue and every day the air conditioner rattled and sputtered, and she prayed it wouldn't break down altogether because they really couldn't afford to fix it. Every day except today, of course. It wouldn't be her problem soon.

Bruno reached for her and slurred, "Come on now, it's not time to get up yet" which she correctly interpreted as "let's fuck", and mentally sighed, preparing for another round of inept grabbing and pounding and occasionally, pain.

He rolled onto her, his wet mouth sucking at her cheek, having missed her mouth entirely, and she flinched as stale breath whooshed over her, smelling intriguingly of whiskey and popcorn. He yanked up her nightie. She opened her legs and there was a stretch of fumbling as he tried to enter her, but he couldn't. She lay still.

"Come on," he muttered, rubbing himself, trying to get hard, his hand banging uselessly against her thigh.

"It's okay," she whispered, but perhaps she shouldn't have said anything at all. His hand shot from his limp dick to her throat, and he shook her, before clipping the side of her face. It had all happened so fast that she didn't have time to move aside, and the blow made her eyes water. She scrambled away from him, out of bed, out of reach, and he collapsed back onto the rumpled sheets.

"Your fault," he told her. "Ugly bitch. Whore."

3

She crouched in between the bed and the wall, the sting of his words hurting more than the slap did, as they always did. There was a gurgling snore and she let out a shaky breath, her hand creeping up to cradle her throbbing cheek.

The light coming through the window had turned from grey to golden, and the glass looked as though it was rippling - but no, it was the air outside. It was shimmering, turning the view of next door's oak trees into a hazy mist, with tendrils of fog creeping out of the shadowy places among the leaves. She squinted. It was as though there were a pair of eyes looking at her, as green as emeralds, turning her inside out.

She shook her head, clearing it. The slap must've been harder than she'd thought.

She waited a few minutes more before crawling out and grabbing her clothes, placed ready on the rocking chair. She changed in the bathroom, snuck back into the room, filched his jeans and jacket, and went through his pockets in the hallway. Usually, she only took the coins and small crumpled notes, the ones he was less likely to notice, but this time, the last time, she took the lot, fifty-seven dollars and eighty-five cents. She slipped the wallet in her pocket too, intending to dump it in a bin in town.

Back in the bedroom, she dropped his clothes on the floor where he'd left them. Next—and this was the bit she'd lovingly turned over in her mind for days now—she took his phone, held it to his face to unlock it, and swiped a hard factory reset. She replaced the phone in his jacket pocket and scuttled out the door, heart pounding so hard she could hear the blood thrumming in her ears, her smile so wide it made her swollen jaw ache.

The car started first try, which she took as a good omen. She drove to the swimming complex and parked under the largest tree, ostensibly for shade, but the weather was so warm it was likely pointless. The beater wasn't actually hers. It belonged to Bruno, and she'd known about the tracker tucked into the spare tyre compartment for months now. He wouldn't notice anything different—if he could even get into his phone to check on her at all. Ember was just going to work as she always did.

There was enough time to loosen up with a few lengths of the main pool, and she soon settled into a rhythm. Her mind drifted as her body ploughed up and down the lane, muscles flexing and straining, heart pumping. Swimming was always a release, a time of liminal space between the heavy burden of home and the energetic bubbly time spent at work.

Her new art school wasn't far from the coast. Maybe she could take a trip to the beach and swim in the ocean. She'd never seen the ocean in real life before, never tasted its salt on her lips, never fought for balance against relentless, pounding waves. Her money wouldn't go far, though. She couldn't go spending it all on day-tripping and excursions. She'd have to get a job somewhere, a room in a boarding house, maybe. Her hard-won scholarship would pay for her fees and there was enough left over to pay for basic food and utilities, but to have some kind of life, she'd need to get a part-time job.

Too keyed up to finish her customary thirty laps, she got out of the pool and went to the changing room to put on her swim instructor tee. Although her cheek still felt tender, she couldn't see a mark in the mirror. There was nothing to say that Bruno had laid hands on her again. She was grateful for that. Explaining bruises away was easy but strained the limits of belief sometimes. The sympathetic looks from her colleagues made her feel uneasy, as if she were wrong somehow, not quite fitting into the world like they did.

The other swim instructors arrived and then Jan, as hard-faced and volatile as her cousin Bruno, conducted the morning meeting. It was because of her that Ember had bothered coming in at all. If she'd ditched work altogether, Jan would call Bruno, wanting to know where she was. But today, Ember's last two students had cancelled. Jan didn't know. Ember hadn't told her. And with the busy crowd of students, and teachers in identical swim uniforms, she wouldn't notice Ember had gone. That was an extra two hours to make her escape. She'd left her bag stowed in her padlocked locker, and there was nothing in there to alarm anyone at first glance anyway: a change of clothes, a kit with her favourite paint brushes and tools, and, tucked deep inside an inner pocket, a cheap burner phone with her bus and plane tickets carefully loaded. Of course, if they looked any closer, they'd also find close to a thousand dollars in cash she'd saved from selling paintings and stealing from Bruno's pockets. Not enough, but enough.

The nervous excitement that had been bubbling inside her all day kept her alert and happy, even as she threw sinking weights for the kids to dive for, dragged gleeful littlies around by pool noodles, and gently corrected her adult swimmers who'd learned so many bad habits that they were harder to teach than the children. When the last lesson of the day was done, she slipped away, got dressed, and headed out the door. She took the back way out of the complex, leaving her car with the tracker parked out the front. Freedom, she decided, smelled like chlorine and hot asphalt.

She pulled her cap low over her eyes, and with her head down, made her way down the street. Twenty minutes until her bus left; she was cutting it fine. She sped up, got to the intersection, and looked both ways. There was a noise, a familiar throaty roar that made the hairs on her arms stand up, and then an old orange Mustang with the ding on its front fender nosed its way around the corner.

Bruno.

CHAPTER 2

Fuck, fuck, fuck.

She spun and took off down the street, backpack thumping against her ribs, but he'd already seen her.

"Ember! Get back here!"

The aggrieved shout spurred her, and she picked up speed, sneakers slapping against the hot pavement. Her breath came hard and fast, her body already tired from a restless night and a day of swimming, pushing itself into new heights of physical exertion by adrenaline, fear and anger.

Around the corner, and across someone's yard, down a narrow side street and through an alley into a cul-de-sac, blocked at one end by an enormous house. Shit. She edged behind a large maple tree and peered down the street. Nothing. Heat shimmers rose from the pavement, making her blink. For an instant it had seemed as if the entire world had quavered, become hazy and indistinct, before it came back into sharp relief again.

She leaned against the tree, trying to catch her breath, before swinging her bag off her back and digging around for her phone. Ten minutes until the bus left. She wasn't much closer to the station than she had been before. She needed to get a move on. At least if she were at the station, he couldn't very well drag her off the bus in front of witnesses, could he? She just needed to get there.

Her head snapped up. There was a consumptive throbbing in the air, growing louder and louder. She risked a peek past the tree trunk. At the end of the street, the orange mustang rolled slowly past. Ember glimpsed Bruno peering down the street and she dodged back out of sight, closing her eyes in silent appeal. When she risked another look back, the car had gone, the invasive engine noise slowly fading to nothing.

She was so focused on Bruno that the tremor under her feet barely registered at first. She paused, uncertainly, resting a hand against the tree trunk for balance in case the earth chose to move even more vigorously. Was that an earthquake? She looked up at the branches overhead, wondering if it was safer to shelter under the tree or out on the pavement away from the houses, and then, as the earth gave another tremor, darted into the middle of the road.

The temperature change from the shade of the leafy tree to the unforgiving black of the road was considerable. Houses all around, new builds all of them, expensive houses for expensive people, shimmered in the heat. The wavering air became hazier, thicker, almost viscous. Tendrils of white mist rose from the tarmac, like steam from a kettle, coalescing into a pulsating ball of cloud stretching high into the sky.

Ember gaped in bewilderment at the roiling, billowing mass in front of her, and then dropped her bag and clapped her hands over her ears as, with a deafening scraping of nails on a chalkboard, the cloud tore itself in half.

A man stepped out of the void, tall and lithe, with blond hair and angular features, wearing an outlandish costume the colour of pale golden buckskin that flowed and ebbed around his body like water. He blinked at her and as a slow smile spread across his face, she felt a tugging deep in the pit of her stomach.

There came another ear-splitting ripping, and she whirled. A second dense mist, black and oily, had formed behind her and was steadily tearing itself in two to reveal another man, dark-haired and black eyed. He wore what looked like a military uniform, velvet smooth in ebony black with mottled silver buttons and shoulder straps, and a sword—a sword!—at his hip.

He looked past Ember as though she was too insignificant to warrant even a glance. "Now, now, cousin." His voice was both lazy and menacing. "No one likes a cheater."

He held up a steadily revolving ball of orange, of *fire,* and then he threw. The fireball whizzed past Ember, so close that a streak of heat seared her cheek. There was the unpleasant smell of singed hair, and then something cannoned into the small of her back, sending her sprawling to the ground.

CHAPTER 3

She struggled, and the weight on her back lifted as the blond man dragged her unceremoniously to her feet.

"Are you hurt?" He raised a gentle hand to her cheek, a finger tracing the path that had felt the touch of the fireball. Without waiting for an answer, he whirled on the other man, pushing her behind him. "How now, Ashe. You know Earth, and everything about her, is sacrosanct."

Ashe's glance skated over her dismissively, and he lifted his hands in surrender. He scoffed in either resignation or disgust, Ember couldn't tell. "You know full well I was aiming at you."

"I doubt the Adjudicator would see it that way. Perhaps you need to work on your aim."

Ashe's face darkened, and another ball of fire appeared in his hand. He held it up with a scowl. "Perhaps I do."

The blond man didn't show any sign of fear. Instead, he laughed, genuine amusement on his face. "Try it."

The inertia that had gripped Ember's body—*shock*—receded, and she edged backwards, wanting to put as much distance between her and that ball of fire as possible. She wasn't sure what was happening, but she knew she didn't want to be in the middle of some shoot-out with fireworks, or whatever the hell was going on. *And that freaky mist that had torn a hole in the world?* She blocked that out. She had a bus to catch.

Another step and another, and then she spun, about to run, when the fireball soared over her head, hit the ground, and exploded. It sent up a roaring wall of flame across the road, blocking her path.

Ember screamed, covering her head with her hands. She scrambled back, collided with the blond man, and lost her balance. He slid an arm around her, steadying her, and for an instant their eyes met. His, an intense green dancing with amusement, and hers, a wide-eyed amber filled with bewilderment. He smiled again, slow and sweet, as though he had all the time in the world, as if a maniac chucking fireballs at them mattered not a jot.

"Get away from her, Cole," Ashe warned, his expression as dark and foreboding as the uniform he wore.

"No."

"I'm warning you."

"And I accept your warning."

Ashe gave a grunt of derision and stepped back into the black fog, the wall of fire on the street abruptly vanishing. The cloud closed around Ashe like a zip closing in a cacophony of crackling static that made Ember wince, before swirling and dissipating so quickly it was as though it hadn't been there at all. But there was the other fog bank still billowing nearby, and through the drifts, a glimpse of towering trees and green hills ...

The mass eddied, obscuring her view, and then Cole was in front of her, taking up all her attention. She became acutely aware of his scent, as warm and sultry as cinnamon and leather and grass after the rain. She raised her eyes to him, and his searing gaze immediately drew her in, giving her the impression she had just been scorched by another fireball.

"I have to go," she said, faintly. There were too many questions jostling in her head, the loudest of which was, *what the fuck is going on?* But greater than the desire to ask was the need to run and run and never look back. She shoved at the arm still holding her, wondering if he would let her go, and what she would do if he didn't, and then felt almost disappointed when his arm fell away from her waist.

He stepped back and gave a courtly, old-fashioned bow. "Forgive me and my cousin for scaring you. It was naught, but a game gone awry. He meant you no harm."

Ember swallowed. She couldn't think of anything to say to that. How could he speak so easily, so fluently, when behind him was smoke leading to ... Her eyes widened. A *castle* stood on a distant hill, complete with turrets and flags. The mist whirled, and it vanished.

"I have to go," she repeated, edging around him.

"What is your name?"

"Uh..."

Usually, when a random stranger asked for her name, she would pull a fake one out of the air: Dolores, Natalie, Cynthia, Rose, anything. But the only thing that came out was the truth, "Ember Bailey."

"Ember," he echoed, as though her name pleased him. He said something else, but an orange car approaching at speed drowned out his voice.

The car came to a screeching halt and when Bruno threw open the door and stepped out, Ember almost took off toward him. Bruno, although a tedious, abusive brute, was familiar. She could deal with Bruno. She wasn't sure she could deal with fireballs and castles in the fog and gorgeous men with a death wish.

"What the fuck?" Bruno muttered, taking in first the fog, then the stranger, and then her. "Get in the car, Ember."

The notion of running to Bruno for help vanished. "No."

Bruno took a step toward her, and then stopped, clearly confused by the roiling cloud of white fog in the middle of the road. "Ember, get in the car, or I call the cops."

"What?"

He grinned without mirth. "You stole from me."

The glaring truth of that statement was so banal after everything she'd just experienced that his threats seemed as empty as air.

"I didn't steal anything." Her tone was hard. "I *earned* it."

"We'll let the cops sort that out, shall we?"

He eyed Cole, calculating, and Ember could tell he was weighing up whether he could take Cole in a fight. Bruno often settled differences of opinion that way. He was heavy and stocky, but he was also quick, and he didn't believe in fighting fair.

Cole turned his back on Bruno with a casual disregard, and Bruno's face darkened. Bruno hated being ignored.

"Ember," said Cole, and again, it was as though the two of them were merely strolling down a summer lane or picnicking by a lazy river. "Do you wish to go with him?"

Ember shook her head emphatically. Bruno's face grew red.

"Friend," Cole said to Bruno, in a tone that suggested he considered Bruno the exact opposite. "She says not."

"Who the fuck asked you?" Bruno roared. "Ember, get the fuck in the car *now.*"

He reached behind him, and to Ember's horror, drew out a knife from his pocket and held it out, light glinting off the blade. His bellicose attitude became smugly superior, and he grinned. "Cut you both up."

"Bruno, put that away!" Ember's voice shook. "Don't be stupid."

Typical, she thought irrelevantly. This close to fulfilling the dream of a lifetime, and it was all falling to pieces because of a jealous bully and a ...

She looked up at Cole. His flirtatious green gaze had become like flint, sending a thrill of fear down her back. *What was he?* There was something suddenly menacing about Cole, something cold and unfeeling, an aura of absolute indifference permeating his entire being. It wasn't hate, or anything remotely like it. That would have at least been something. This was an absence, a void, a dearth of humanity. This was what death was like. Ember shuddered. Bruno's jaw grew slack, the knife dangling from his fingers. He had felt it too.

"Run," Ember whispered.

There was a pause in the movement of the world. The breeze dropped. The birds stopped singing. Even Ember's heart seemed to take an agonisingly long time between beats. And in that moment, Cole raised a hand, and Bruno collapsed in on himself like a dying star, an implosion of flesh, clothing, hair, muscle, and tendons, his innards suddenly outward, and then there was nothing, but a bloody ball of smoking burnt meat on the road, the knife lying uselessly beside it.

Ember gulped and gagged. Her knees shook uncontrollably, but before she could sag to the ground in a dead faint, Cole slid his arm around her. The fog closed around them both, and they were gone.

CHAPTER 4

There was a sensation of softness like cotton wool, and she floated there for a time, before falling into a dream of dizzying fragments that flew past her like shards of glass on the wind, the mirrored pieces reflecting a sly smile with piercing green eyes, great columns of stone, and fractured colours of fire.

She sat bolt upright, gasping, her forehead clammy with sweat, her heart pounding.

The light was dim, and at first, she had a confused feeling that she'd imagined it all, that she was waking up in her own room and Bruno wasn't home yet. And yet ... and yet this room looked nothing like her cramped space. This room was immense. Wooden beams arched high overhead. Vines of green climbed the stone walls and large windows stood open to admit a warm, fragrant breeze. A sparkling chandelier hung from the ceiling, and white candles in gold holders burned with flames that dipped and wavered, sending shadows crawling across the room.

She drew the sheets to her throat in a rustle of silk, looking wildly this way and that, and then, noticing something felt strange, peeked under the sheet to find that she was naked.

What the —

She blinked, ground her eyes with the palms of her hands, looked again. She had to be dreaming, but somehow this didn't feel like a dream. Pulling the sheet off the bed, she wrapped it around herself and, somewhat restrained by the fabric, waddled clumsily toward the window. Maybe she was in a hospital. Maybe a car had hit her as she was running from Bruno, or she'd had a cramp while swimming, and this was just an elaborate hallucination brought on by the heat, her injuries, and prescription medications. The memory of fog and fireballs nudged her, but she forced it out. That too must have been a hallucination, caused by the pressure and adrenalin of her escape. She could bet if she looked out the window, she'd see a carpark with a sign reading, 'Medical Centre', and then an efficient nurse in a crisp uniform would present her with a bill that she couldn't afford to pay.

But when she leaned on the sill and gazed outside, there was no carpark, nothing to indicate she was in a medical facility of any kind. Instead, it looked as though she was on an upper floor of a hotel in a formal park. A formal mosaic of gardens lay around a fountain with a white statue of a fantastical two-headed creature. Tall hedges separated the grounds from the countryside beyond, placid green pastures and hills stretching out to the horizon. Jagged mountains cut across the skyline to the left, and to the right lay a darker patch of green that looked like it might be jungle. A gentle twilight lay over the scene, and the breeze held the scent of something sultry and mysterious, a vaguely familiar musk that reminded her of leather, cinnamon, and rain. Iridescent white roses on leafy vines twined around the window frame and—she flinched in surprise—there were *things* darting in and out of the flowers, little glowing things that looked like ...

She took a couple of steps back, hand over her mouth, trying to control her breathing, to stifle the panic welling up inside her. She was about to lose it, she knew it. The flying things looked like ... looked like ...

There was a gentle cough behind her, and Ember gave a yelp of fright, spinning to see a girl a few years younger standing behind her, holding a bundle and a tray.

"I apologise for frightening you." Her voice was low and gentle, her accent unremarkable, and she looked frightened herself, as if she thought Ember might lash out and strike her.

"Where am I?" Ember said. "Where the hell are my clothes? And my bag? There was money in it."

The girl blinked, clearly overwhelmed by all the questions being fired at her, and she hastily placed the tray on an ornately carved table near the window before holding out the bundle to Ember. It turned out to be a swishy pink gauze dress threaded with gold that gathered under the bust before falling to the floor. The thin shoulder straps were so delicate they looked as if they couldn't possibly support the weight of the fabric, and when she smoothed the skirt between her fingers, it was so soft and sheer it felt like there was nothing there at all.

"You want me to wear this?" The dress looked as though it would have cost more than a month's rent. "But what about my stuff?"

"Eat first. I know this must be confusing for you." She turned away, evidently waiting for Ember to get herself organised, and Ember let the sheet drop, drawing the dress over her head.

"Any underwear to go with this?" Ember said, fighting her arms free and tugging the dress into place. "Or am I just going commando?"

The girl didn't answer, merely picking up the discarded sheet and heading for the bed.

"You don't have to make it," said Ember, remorseful at making a mess in such a beautiful room. "I'll do it."

"Eat," the girl repeated, and set about repairing the bed covers.

Ember approached the tray. Now that she thought about it, she was starving. The sandwich she'd eaten during her lunch hour seemed a long time ago now. She'd felt too excited and apprehensive to eat any more than that, and now the mere sight of food was enough to set her stomach growling.

The tray held a few scalloped dishes with an array of strange little nibbly things. Black-skinned fruit with orange flesh on one plate, white cheese on another, and another with slices of cold pink meat. There was a pile of bread cut into thin triangles, with an odd purple paste to one side. She hadn't seen food quite like this before and she hesitated, her hand hovering over the dishes, unsure which to try first. It didn't really matter. They were all delicious, even the purple paste, which seemed to be some kind of mashed up vegetable, a bit like avocado in texture, but with a tangy fermented flavour.

As she ate, she watched the girl tidying the bed and fluffing up the pillows. She wore a long dress too, a little shorter and narrower than Ember's, in a nondescript pale green that did nothing for her creamy complexion, dark hair smoothed back under a matching cap. She gave a funny little skip as she reached for a pillow, and stumbled, glancing at Ember as if to check that Ember hadn't noticed.

To gloss over the awkward moment, Ember said, "What's your name?"

The girl looked startled and then, as if no one had ever asked her name before, she ventured, "Lily, my lady."

"Call me Ember, please. And this place? What's the story?"

With her hunger sated, her mind had taken on some sense of clarity. First the earthquake, the weird fog and the fireballs, followed by Bruno —she dragged her mind away from the hunk of steaming meat on the road and moved on—and this gorgeous place and the strange food and the ... yes, the freaking *fairies* fluttering about in the weird sparkling roses, not to mention the fact that she had pinched herself numerous times now and rather than waking up, had just given herself several bruises on her forearms, well, all this could only mean one thing. "Am I dead? Is this heaven?"

Lily looked taken aback at that and shook her head. "This is the castle of the Kingdom of Swords."

Riiiight.

CHAPTER 5

"The Kingdom of Swords? What's that?"

"The prince will explain, I'm sure. He has requested an audience once you're refreshed."

Prince. Swords. Kingdom. It was all too much. Ember sucked in a couple of deep, shuddering breaths. It was going to be fine. She'd see the ... the *prince* ... and ask to go home and that would be that. No need to panic. And in the meantime, she could just enjoy the wonderful weirdness of it all. The food was good, and Lily seemed nice. It was going to be fine.

Lily brought Ember a bowl of warm, scented water to wash her fingers, and a soft towel. She would have dried Ember's fingers too, if Ember hadn't taken the towel from her. Afterwards, Lily adjusted Ember's skirts, and ignoring her protests, tugged the bodice down to expose more of her décolletage, explaining that was how the dress was to be worn.

Ember felt like a player about to take the stage, but she suffered through the primping of her outfit, and then the brushing and pinning of her long dark hair, not wanting to hinder Lily. There were no mirrors, and so she could only guess at what Lily was doing as she piled Ember's hair on top of her head and pulled a few tendrils down around her temples.

Ember asked if there were shoes to match, and Lily looked momentarily flustered, before opening a cupboard, empty save for a pair of soft satin slippers that matched the dress perfectly. When Lily had finished and pronounced her done, Ember followed her out the door.

Her room was at the end of a corridor lined with panels of dark cherry coloured wood, tall candle holders with room for twenty candles lighting the way. This corridor led to another corridor, and then they turned into a wider hallway. Now and then, they passed others moving in the opposite direction, each of whom first stared at Ember and then almost immediately dropped their gaze, as if they were too frightened to stare.

The first time someone walked past, Ember assumed they wore an elaborate headdress of green and purple feathers, but as she turned to watch them pass, she saw it was *wings*, arching up from the shoulder blades, high into the air and then bowing down to trail along the floor. She stopped in her tracks, watching them glide down the hall. When she had collected her wits, Lily was just vanishing around a corner. Ember scampered to catch her up.

There were more people here, some with wings, some without. Once she felt a draught blowing the stray tendrils around her face, and she looked up to see someone flying overhead, as casually as if they were walking. Ember had to work to keep her mouth from gaping open, but there was no doubt about it. She was overwhelmed and overwrought, with too many unfamiliar sights, sounds, smells and tastes, assailing her senses. She wanted nothing more than to run back to her room and crawl into that big, comfortable bed and pull the covers over her head. Or, failing that, find the nearest corner, sink down, clutch her knees and rock. But Lily was striding on, and Ember had no choice but to follow.

They passed under an elaborately carved archway. Lily said, "This is a common archway," but didn't elaborate, and the question Ember had on her lips died almost immediately as they entered an overgrown forest. A faint dirt path wound in between thick stands of trees, bushes, and ferns. Vines dripped from the branches, and under the trees lay a soft carpet of moss, speckled with white starry flowers. The shades of green were calming, comforting, and Ember felt her fingers itch, the familiar longing of wanting to pick up a brush and fill an empty canvas.

She thought they must have left the castle and come into the grounds, but then they passed a still pool of water reflecting sunset clouds, all pinks and yellows, and she discovered the sky was just painted on the ceiling and the forest was still indoors. The water rippled as they went past, and Ember paused, half expecting a fish to leap out of the water, but the ripples stilled unnaturally quickly, and she continued on.

A glimpse through the trees showed a space where the forest hadn't entirely taken over, a space with four stone columns rising high. On one column was an engraving of what looked like three drops of water, on another, a curling fern frond. She didn't have time to see the others because Lily was hurrying on.

"The common areas are open to all," Lily said, indicating another archway beyond, "but that leads to Prince Cole's domain and his ballroom."

The forest abruptly ended as they passed beneath the arch, and they were back in another hallway. It ended in wooden doors carved with two crossed swords and guarded by two men in silver armour, leather gloved hands resting on the sword pommels at their sides. As one, they moved aside as she and Lily approached, and the doors swung open.

Music swelled and Ember caught an intriguing glimpse of whirling movement inside. Lily gestured for Ember to enter. Ember did so, looking back at Lily, who hadn't moved over the threshold, realising belatedly that the only person she knew in this place was letting her go on alone. She turned back, but the doors had already closed behind her, and she had no choice but to face the prince by herself.

CHAPTER 6

M usic, wild and tempestuous, filled the air, a cacophony that her brain couldn't seem to organise. There was a beat and rhythm to it she recognised, something elemental and instinctual that spoke to her deep in her gut, but the melody was a collection of garish notes that didn't appear to make any kind of sense to Ember, who was more accustomed to pop music. But even if she had been a student of classical or orchestral music, this still would have sounded - *off* - tainted, disturbing. She couldn't tell where it was coming from; there were no speakers jutting out from the walls, no band hidden from sight behind a screen.

Half-naked dancers filled the ballroom, beautiful young men and women, all lean muscle and flowing hair, their lithe bodies bending and twisting to the beat. Wisps of smoky black fabric barely concealed taut flesh as the dancers moved. People, if you could call them that, thronged the room, some perched on velvet couches and some standing, chatting idly, and rocking to the music. They were clad in rich colours; many with flowing dresses like Ember's, elaborate jewellery glinting on fingers, wrists and throats, and others in military-style uniforms half concealed by capes and hoods. All were watching the dancers and talking behind their hands, and none paid any attention to Ember.

Silver clad guards stood in strategic positions around the hall. Behind their metal helmets, their eyes glittered as they observed those in the room, watchful and alert. At the head of the ballroom stood a dais with a single white throne that shone like the inside of a shell, and on the throne sprawled a familiar figure.

Cole.

As she recognised him, her heart thumped a little harder in her chest. Even from this distance, she felt his presence as a physical thing, could once again smell the scent of him, a fragrance that permeated the entire hall, warm and enticing. Under the candlelight, his fair countenance was striking, his hair much whiter blond than she remembered, his skin almost seeming to glow. Across the crowd, their eyes caught and held, and she felt her cheeks flush and a pleasant ache worked its way through her body, making her wish she was wearing underwear. It was a physical reaction she hadn't been prepared for and it flustered her. She backed away, determined to leave, and head back to the relative safety of her room, and Cole rose to his feet.

At once, the music stopped. Unnaturally fast, the dancers immediately ceased their gyrations and sank down to one knee. Conversation stilled. All was silent. Ember froze, wanting to sink through the floor, as one by one, the people around the room turned to stare at her.

Cole gave a flick of a hand. The dancers rose, moved seamlessly into line, and filed out of the room through a set of doors toward the rear of the room. They passed closely to Ember, and she smiled at them politely, but none even acknowledged her; their eyes fixed on the floor. Up close, their features were strong and angular, with high cheekbones, full crimson lips, and strangely pointed ears. They looked as if they had all come out of the same box off the same production line, with little variation between them. All were stunning, all were tall and fit, all were fair-haired with light complexions. Their eyes, however, were dull, and they appeared tired and morose.

The doors closed behind them and the groups of people in the room resumed their chatting and laughing. It was like a cocktail party of sorts, although there were no drinks or trays of food, and the music had ceased. Now and then, Ember caught one of them staring at her, and then they would gossip to their friends behind their hands.

She wondered if she should walk through them and approach the throne, and what should she do when she got there. Curtsey? Kneel on the ground like the dancers? Wave and say hi? But Cole was already stepping down off the dais and moving forward to her, and so she timidly approached him, uncomfortably aware of the unfamiliar skirts swishing around her legs, the stares of the others, the cool air against her exposed décolletage, the trembling of her hands. But as Cole neared, he gave her an intimate, approving smile, one that took her all in, showing what he thought of her in her new outfit, and her confidence rose.

He took her hands in his and gently kissed her knuckles, his lips barely grazing her fingers, his breath a whisper against her skin, and once again she felt a swooping in her stomach that was pure and physical attraction, the stirring of primal lust. This man did things to her she hadn't felt for... well, ever, really. He looked up at her, his eyes liquid, his mouth arched in a lopsided smile.

"Ember Bailey," he said. "Welcome to my home."

She tried to respond, but all that came out was an embarrassing croak, and so she cleared her throat and tried again, managing a faltering, "Thank you."

He tucked her hand under his arm and walked her to the side of the room, away from the stares of the others. He seemed as easy with her as if he had known her for years, and she couldn't help but lean toward him, arching into the warmth of his body as though she were a cat and he a cosy fireplace, until the vision of a sizzling slab of meat slipped into her head.

She abruptly tugged her hand away, aghast at the way her body had betrayed her so easily, when he had murdered Bruno in cold blood, right in front of her, with just a wave of his hand. This man must be evil. He was certainly not human. And here she was, practically rubbing up against him.

Cole didn't remark on her sudden recoil, merely nodding as though he knew what was on her mind, and confirming it with, "He was going to kill you. I could see it in his mind. And I can't let anyone hurt you, Ember. I won't allow it."

"You don't even know me," Ember said.

He nodded. "No." He leaned toward her and whispered in her ear, low and enticing. "Not yet."

She looked away, trying to control the involuntary response of her body, telling herself sternly, '*you don't know this guy, snap out of it Ember, he's practically kidnapped you for heaven's sake*', and he chuckled, as if he knew exactly the dilemma she was struggling with as her wilful body argued with her brain. He courteously stepped away from her, putting some welcome distance between them, and she felt a measure of control return.

"Is your room and maid to your satisfaction?"

"It's lovely. And Lily is very sweet. Very good at her job," she added. Maybe she could get Lily a pay rise or something. She liked Lily, and besides, she knew what it was like to struggle on minimum wage.

"All my servants are good at their jobs. You only have to ask them for whatever comfort you want."

"What I want is to go home now. Please."

He looked surprised, clearly never having even considered that she might want to leave, and then his brows furrowed. "Why?"

"I've got a scholarship to an art school. It's my chance. It's everything I've ever wanted." She could hear the pleading tone in her voice. Even if he didn't know what she meant—what would a being like him know about scholarships or art schools?—he could surely hear the longing anguish in her voice and would respond to it.

An expression of chagrin flickered across his face. "I'm sorry, Ember. I can't take you back. Not right now."

"But ... why?" Panic rose within her. She had to get back, she had to. She couldn't stay here in this strange place, with fairies and angels and ... her eyes widened as she caught sight of someone in the crowd, someone with wild tawny hair, armour half-shielding a broad chest which ended in what looked like the lower half of a horse's body. *Centaur,* her mind helpfully supplied, and she looked away, not wanting to be caught staring at yet another extraordinary sight.

"You remember my cousin, Ashe?"

Cole's voice dragged her back to the conversation, and she blinked, trying to process his words. Ashe. Of course, the other one, dark as Cole was fair, the one who had thrown fire at her. She nodded.

"We can only tear the veil around Earth together, and Ashe is ... not happy with me right now. He won't help. He enjoys making difficulties for me."

"But what has that got to do with me?" She sounded rude, and she knew it, but she couldn't help it. "Maybe if I asked him, I could persuade him. Can I talk to him?"

"Ashe resides in his rooms in the castle, and none may enter there save with his permission, not even I. Just as no one may enter here without my consent." He took her hand again, and tingles sparked up and down her arm in a rather disconcerting manner. "But you might well see him around in the common areas, and most definitely at the Ball. But I warn you, like many fae, he doesn't like humans."

She could have guessed that already. "But I need to go. I don't belong here."

He lifted a hand and gently brushed a strand of hair away from her face. "I don't know about that," he said lightly. "You belong as much as anyone."

Once again, the intense green of his gaze captured her, threatening to sweep her away, and she could feel herself swaying toward him, tilting her cheek toward his touch...

"Your Highness," came a feminine voice behind her, heavy with sarcasm. "There you are."

CHAPTER 7

T he woman was striking, extraordinarily so, even in this world of beauty and grace. She was slender, with well-defined muscles. Peculiar markings were etched across her pale skin, which looked as though someone had traced scallops across her with a graphite pencil, and then dusted them with shimmering powder. Her long, golden hair fell down her back in shimmering waves, caught up at her temples with sapphire clips that complemented the ocean blue of her gown. Sheer, clinging layers showed off the planes, curves, and dips of her body, and she wore gold circlets around her forehead, throat, and wrists. Every movement she made was like a dancer's, deliberate and elegant, and as she approached them, she slowed her walk so that they had ample time to admire her. She made Ember feel heavy and gauche, as though she had just emerged from the swimming pool, when the buoyancy of water became the relentless pull of gravity.

She didn't acknowledge Ember at first, just walked straight past her, and kissed Cole on the cheek. He slid what seemed like an automatic arm around her waist, and only then did she deign to utter a languid greeting to Ember.

"Hello."

"Hello," Ember echoed.

The woman inspected her closely, taking in Ember's hair, face, shoes, and dress, making Ember feel like a prize pig at the fair. Without taking her eyes off Ember, she addressed Cole, "I apologise for staring, Your Highness. I've just never seen one up close before."

Cole's mouth creased in amusement. "Ember, this is Lissa. Lissa, play nice."

Lissa pouted in a way that showed she quite like the look of her lips when she did so, and said, "I thought you liked the way I played."

They exchanged an intense, intimate glance that told Ember volumes about their relationship. They were clearly lovers, and she was clearly in the way. Feeling stupid, she was about to make her apologies and request to be shown back to her room, when she caught sight of strange markings on Lissa's neck; three creased flaps that opened and closed with every breath she took. Gills. Lissa had *gills*.

"Your Highness is sure to have a fascinating story about why he's brought a human into our midst, just before the tournament," said Lissa, seemingly unaware of Ember's fascination with her neck. "Could it be a strategy which you haven't yet discussed with your teammates? A gift to win over the Adjudicator, perhaps?"

Cole gave her an impatient frown. "She was in danger. I took it upon myself to remove her."

Which wasn't exactly true, Ember thought. He had removed the danger as soon as he had turned Bruno inside-out. But the mention of a tournament piqued her interest. "A tournament?"

"*The* tournament," Lissa said, with a lift of a perfectly arched eyebrow. "The games to determine who will be the Sword, and who will be his Blade. Of course, we all know what the outcome will be," and she gave Cole a smile.

Cole, however, didn't smile back. "The result is far from guaranteed. Both teams are evenly matched." He explained to Ember, "Lissa is on my team, defending our honour in the water, the captain of the Waves."

Well, that explains the gills, Ember thought uncharitably, but aloud she said, "And what is the Blade?"

Lissa let out a peal of laughter, staring at Ember with incredulity.

"She doesn't know," said Cole. "How could she? What do humans know of us?"

"*The* Sword rules all in the Kingdom of Swords," said Lissa. "The other kingdoms must have two sharing rulership, but the Swords are such fearsome warriors we only need one. Whoever loses the tournament will be the Sword's second, his blade to wield, the power inside the throne."

Ember nodded as though she understood, but there was too much to take in and her head was spinning. All she wanted was some quiet and space to absorb everything she'd seen so far.

"Ashe shall be brought to heel," Lissa continued, "and all will be well."

This earned her a smile from Cole, and she blushed prettily, whispering in his ear. He nodded, and she turned to Ember. "Enjoy yourself. The tournament only happens once in a fae lifetime. You will see marvels."

Ember wasn't sure how to respond to this, but it didn't matter. Lissa was already threading her way through the crowd, people falling back from her and whispering in admiration as she passed. She looked as though she was used to attention and liked it, Ember thought. She envied Lissa her lazy air of self-assurance, as though she deserved every single covetous glance. Most of the time, Ember just wanted to fade into the background, unseen, unheard, unchallenged.

"Our leaders get elected," she said. "It's just a big popularity contest."

Cole laughed. "Then the throne is mine already. My cousin is rather ... grim. He can be formidable. But so can we."

He took Ember's hand and tucked it into the crook of his elbow again, walking with her toward the door that the dancers had gone through. "That's how we ended up in Earth. We were arguing over a small rule, and our powers came together and then ..." he made a 'poof!' noise, like an explosion. "It's been happening more often, as the tournament draws near. I'll show you."

The guards standing at the doors bowed as they approached, the doors swung open, and Cole led her through.

CHAPTER 8

T he stone walls echoed their footsteps back to them, and Ember's instinct was to tiptoe and stay quiet. This part of the castle didn't have the welcoming, busy feel of the halls she had already been through. This part was silent, foreboding, watchful. White candles lit their way and occasionally they passed an iron door welded with the symbol of two crossed swords. It was colder here too, a contrast to the sultry warmth she had experienced thus far, as though something was sucking the warmth out of the vicinity.

"The tournament takes days," Cole said conversationally as they walked. "It's a competition played over three elements: water, earth and air."

"And Lissa takes on the water element?"

"Yes. You probably noticed how she's more than adequately adapted for it, being a water sprite."

"I noticed ... something," Ember said, thinking of those peculiar gills opening and closing, and of what she now understood were shimmering scales covering her body.

"And the winner of all gets to take the fire element, and the King-dom," he said. "It's just up here."

They halted in front of another door, similar to all the others, but instead of the crossed swords emblem, the door displayed an iron moulding of a leafy tree. Cole turned the handle, and they entered.

The room was sunlit and airy, the opposite of what she'd seen of the palace so far, with arching windows overhead. From the twilight view from her room, she had assumed it was much, much later in the day, and the switch in time momentarily confused her, but the sight in the middle of the room chased that thought away just as quickly as it had come.

It was a tree, an impossible tree, towering high in the centre of the room, with spreading branches and leaves of fire. The flames crackled and glowed, giving off a pulsating heat that she could feel from the doorway. On the opposite side of the room was another door leading out, but she wasn't sure anyone could make it past the tree without getting singed.

"This is the heart of the kingdom." Cole pointed to something set into the trunk of the tree, which Ember had to squint to see, the flames making it difficult to discern. It was an orange jewel with a gold filigree surround and a chain hanging from it. The reflection of the flames made the stone glimmer and sparkle, looking as if it were turning and twisting, as if it were alive. "Whoever wins the tournament can take the pendant. The new Sword will wear it, and the Blade shall be imprisoned within it."

Despite the warmth, Ember felt a chill crawl down her back. Cole smiled and drew her out of the room, carefully closing the door. "And that's why I need to win."

The stone walls of the corridor were welcome after the heat of the fiery tree, and she made no protest when Cole asked if she'd like to see the gardens. Fresh cool air would be welcome.

The door at the end of the hall led to the outside, not into the formal gardens and fountain that Ember had seen from her room, but a different part of the grounds, with manicured green lawns and a sloping hill that led down to a wooded area. The sun shone brightly and again she felt that disconcerting sense of time displacement as she adjusted. Perhaps this was what jet lag felt like, she thought.

Behind her, the castle rose into the sky, a fairytale concoction of grey stone, flowering vines, turrets and spires, the castle she had seen in the fog. A racetrack lay to one side, fenced with white railings, with horses galloping round and round, the thudding of the hooves against the turf a rhythmical backdrop.

"They're training." Cole indicated the horses with a nod of his head and Ember did a double take when she realised they weren't horses at all. They were centaurs, like the one she had seen in the ballroom, bare-chested and wild, shouting to one another. Some carried bows and arrows, others had spears, and all were shooting and slashing at various targets around the track. "The first game is Earth. They will race. Some will die."

The matter-of-fact way he said it and the memory of Bruno's demise still fresh in her mind, made Ember's skin crawl. "They would die for you?"

Cole shrugged. "They are my conduit. My magic will run through their veins. If they die, a piece of me dies too. So, in a way, I suppose I'm dying for them as much as they're dying for me."

"Brutal," murmured Ember, and then blushed as she realised she had spoken her thought aloud, but Cole didn't seem to mind.

"This is the way of the Fae," Cole said, still focusing on the centaurs, his tone absentminded. "To enjoy everything, as much as we can get, until we're stuffed with it. We're gluttons of our own appetites, uncaring of consequences. We live, we love, we kill, we die. What more is there?"

Ember couldn't answer that. There was a strange appeal to it, this hedonistic life where nothing mattered but one's own satisfaction. No bills to pay, no comparison of life and status, no menial work, no responsibility. And then she thought of Lily, and of the morose dancers, and of whoever had made her food and clothes, and she guessed Cole was speaking of his own life, without consideration of the others who made up his world. It was easy to be hedonistic when you were at the top of the pile, Ember thought. Fae or human, the rich and powerful were the same everywhere.

"Would you like to sit?" Cole said, turning his attention away from the track and back to Ember. She coloured a little under his steady gaze and smoothed her skirts.

"I don't want to get my dress dirty. It's the prettiest one I've ever worn."

A frown flickered across his face as though dirt was something he'd never considered before in his life, and then he smiled. "Permit me," and gestured toward the bottom of the slope.

Ember blinked. She was certain that the fringed picnic blanket, fully laid out with cushions and food, wine glasses and a silver wine bucket, as well as a little vase stuffed with red roses, hadn't been there earlier. She would have noticed. Cole led her down the hill and they settled on the blanket. Ember took her slippers off and tucked her bare feet underneath her, wondering if it would be rude to ask Cole to magic her up a pair of sneakers. Her slippers were pretty, but hardly practical for outdoors.

He poured from a bottle of wine and handed her a glass. The frosted liquid was delicious, the bubbles dancing on her tongue. She leaned back into the cushions, hardly able to believe that this was her, Ember Bailey, once barely scraping by and living with an abusive brute, now relaxing beside a flamboyant castle while the handsomest man she had ever seen in her life poured her wine and gazed at her as though she were the most fascinating person in the world.

"Tell me about yourself," Cole said. "Beautiful Ember Bailey, pursued by angry men, destined for art school, and ..." his voice trailed off and he looked embarrassed. "That's all I know."

She laughed. The wine was fizzing through her veins, and she felt light and happy. "There's not much more, believe me."

"Did you grow up in that town?" he asked.

"No. I've been there for... five years now? My parents died when I was young, and then I got put into the system, you know, and as soon as I could, I left and ended up there. But I was planning on leaving. Literally. I was on my way when you showed up."

She raised her glass and took a sip, trying to cover her nerves, but her hand was shaking a little. She didn't enjoy talking about her past. It was like a series of photographic slides, slotting into her memory as if on a projector, glimpses of new schools, angry foster parents, ill-fitting clothes, hunger sometimes, social workers, other kids as lost as she was. But she was tired of all of that. It was time for paintings, not photographs, for her life to have meaning. She wanted to be a glutton of her own appetite. She wanted to paint and get lost in the art of her creation; to make something that meant something. She wanted a place of her own, a place where she mattered. Art school would lead to that place, she was sure of it.

"How did they die?" Cole said. His tone was gentle, and she gave him a wan smile.

"Car crash. The car went up in flames and … yeah. They pulled me out, but my parents were already dead."

A momentary frown creased his brow, and she wondered at that. But then he was leaning close, his thumb brushing away a tear that she wasn't even aware had fallen. "Don't cry, Ember."

"I'm not." She'd come to terms with her parents dying a long time ago, and in fact, she couldn't even remember a time when she *had* cried about it. Maybe when she was small. But her memories of that time were blurry. She couldn't remember anything clearly. But the pressure of Cole's flesh against hers was triggering a familiar tingle, and faint veins of pleasure were pulsating through her. She pulled back, suddenly remembering Lissa. Ember Bailey might be capable of a few dodgy things, but she did not mess with other people's property, no matter how much she …

Far from looking cross at her physical rejection of him, Cole looked amused, as if he had just discovered something new, something challenging. A sly smile creased the corners of his mouth and then he leaned forward, sliding a hand behind her hair, and pulling her close. He brought her to him, their lips just a hairsbreadth apart. The pleasurable tingles were sparking rapidly now, and she could feel something dark and heated in her gut, spreading down between her legs, turning her liquid. Lissa was nothing. Lissa was gone. It was Ember who filled that minute distance, she who brushed her lips against his, and taking up the invitation, he dragged her closer, his arms tight around her, his mouth on hers. She gave herself up to him in that moment, hungrily accepting his lips, his tongue, his breath, unable to stop a soft moan of desire as she clung to him. His hand snaked up her body to brush lightly against her breast, before pinching a hard nipple through the gauzy chiffon, making her gasp against his mouth with surprised pleasure and pain, and earning a soft growl of approval in return.

"Better watch out, cousin," came a lazy voice, cutting through the mist of Ember's rising passion, "Or Lissa will not be pleased."

CHAPTER 9

E mber pushed away from Cole, hand to her swollen lips, trying to recover herself. She felt as if someone had just chucked a bucket of water over her, dousing her building heat. So, Cole was with Lissa. She knew it. Besides, Cole wasn't even *human*. Surely, she thought, she had to draw a line *some*where.

She shuffled back into the cushions and tried to look as though she were invisible, but she needn't have bothered. Cole and the newcomer's attention was on each other, and as their conversation continued above her head, eventually she regained wits enough to look up. Her eyes widened as she recognised him, and she ducked her head, in case he remembered her and tried to kill her again.

Ashe. She remembered him as a terrifying shadow in black, hurling fire at her head, but here now, in the placid stillness of the afternoon light, he didn't look quite as monstrous. Still, he had a stern bearing, the antithesis of Cole, as grim as Cole was playful, with jet black hair, black eyes and a dark complexion. His skin had an undertone of something to it, something that looked like fragrance oil floating in warm water, the iridescence of a shell or a raw opal, with faint rainbow colours visible just beneath the brown surface of his skin. There was a wildness to him that the strict, polished uniform of black leather with metal trimmings that he wore couldn't conceal, an air of untamed danger, of a predator.

"... and what on earth will that accomplish, spying on my team, Ashe?" Cole was saying, with a knowing smile, as if the thought didn't phase him at all. "Swirl won't stand for that. He'll count it as an insult to his honour. And I'm not sure you want to earn the wrath of Swirl."

Ashe gave a scoffing grunt. "I'm fully aware of the capabilities of your team. There's nothing new to learn. And I put my faith in Tinth to manage Swirl."

Cole's green eyes sharpened and his tone became stilted, although why, Ember couldn't imagine. "*My* team. *My* blood. *I* will manage Swirl."

Ashe shrugged carelessly, but there was a smug set to his bearing, as if knowing full well he had needled Cole and received exactly the reaction he wanted.

Ember hardly understood any of this byplay, and she shrank back as Ashe's dark gaze skated over her. "I can't imagine it will thrill Lissa, you fraternising with other fae. You don't want her distracted."

Smug complacency replaced Cole's disgruntled attitude. He gave Ember the ghost of a wink, which brought a flush to her cheeks. "Look again."

Ashe's casual glance became piercing. She heard his indrawn breath, noted the way his voice became tight. "Cole. What have you done? A human?"

"Me?" said Cole with indignation, but there was more than a little amusement in his voice. He was enjoying this. "You're the one who showed up throwing fire at everything. I rescued her."

"There's nothing in the rulebook to prevent fire being thrown on earth," Ashe said, but his tone was uncertain.

"Because the Adjudicator would have assumed that no one would have been stupid enough to do it. You know the rules, Ashe. We are sacrosanct from each other until the tournament. Here, and on Earth."

"I wasn't aiming to kill," Ashe said. "Otherwise, you would be dead."

Cole scoffed at that, his eyes alight with mischief. He's enjoying this, thought Ember, the gleeful joy of a cheeky younger sibling who has finally got one over their serious big brother.

"Our duty is to protect humankind," said Cole. "Surely maiming one of them to make a point doesn't fall under that mandate?"

Ashe gave a growl and turned to Ember. "I apologise if I ... maimed you." Without waiting for a reply, he turned on his heel to go.

"Wait!"

Cole stared at her with an eyebrow lifted, and Ashe turned back. His dark eyes closely raked her from head to toe, and his lip curled as if he didn't much like what he saw.

"Is that how you address a prince?" he enquired glacially. Ember flushed. The lady of the house in her final foster home, a Mrs Fletcher, had been a kindergarten teacher and spoke to everyone in the same manner, as if she were several metres above everyone else. It grated on Ember then, and it grated on her now.

"*Your Highness.*" Sarcasm dripped from her tone, and without giving him time to retort, ploughed on. "I understand that in order to send me back, I need you and your ..." she waved her hand in the air, not knowing exactly what it was he had. Magic? Power? Special talents? "...abilities," she finished. "I'd like to go home. Please."

His expression changed imperceptibly at the word 'please', a narrowing of his eyes and a hint of curiosity in those dark eyes as they moved over her again, deliberately, lingering on the curve of her breasts. A warm flush came unbidden to her cheeks, and she had a sudden desire to tug her dress up to her chin. She tried to keep the dislike from her eyes, injecting a pleading look instead, her fingers crossed for luck, hidden by the folds of her skirts.

"No," he said, and made to leave.

"Why?" she demanded and couldn't help surging to her feet. "You have to! I can't stay here! I've got things to do. I have priorities."

He smiled as he turned back to her, a feral smile that made her think of a panther tearing at bloodied flesh. "Yes," he agreed. "I've seen your priorities. You're lucky that Lissa didn't."

She sucked in an aggrieved breath, only just resisting the childish urge to stamp her foot.

Cole chuckled. "Now, now," he chided, and then to Ember, "Perhaps my cousin doesn't have enough energy left to tear the veil between worlds?"

Ember could tell he meant it as a dig, but to her surprise, Ashe readily acquiesced.

"That's right. I'm spent." He directed his words to Ember. "The games are my ... *priority*. That is my focus. When the tournament concludes, you'll be returned. If you survive that long."

Ember blinked. "What does that mean?"

"Humans are too fragile for fae," he said, looking askance at his cousin. "You need us, but we don't need you. Be careful."

Leaving Ember speechless, he gave her a supercilious bow and strode off toward the castle. On the track, the centaurs came to a halt, chests heaving, spears and bows dangling from languid fingers, eyes hard as they watched him pass. Only when he'd disappeared inside did they return to their training.

Ember sank down onto the blanket again, her fingers restlessly plucking at the fringe on the blanket.

"It's too nice an afternoon to be spoiled by my cousin's petulance," said Cole gently. He picked up a bowl and held it out to her. "Strawberry?"

She took one automatically, but as she crushed the sweet tart berry between her teeth, she couldn't help but linger over Ashe's words. *Humans are too fragile for fae. Be careful.*

What did that mean? And what did that mean for her?

CHAPTER 10

T hey lay out on the blanket for a little while longer, talking. The brief glimpses into Ember's life seemed to fascinate Cole, and his eyes rarely left her face. But she was reluctant to talk about her past. She didn't have many happy memories and thinking about it caused her pain.

Instead, she talked about painting, how she loved messing about with oils and acrylics, and how she had once won an award at school. She told him with pride about the time her paintings had featured in a newspaper article for up-and-coming local artists. No matter that the paper was just a small-town rag, and the readership was in the low thousands. It had been a thrilling moment for her, and she still had a copy of the article stuck carefully between the pages of an old journal.

"The tournament will take up many days," Cole said. "I'll be occupied with training and with my team. But all my servants and rooms are at your disposal. Whatever you wish for is yours. Perhaps you'd like to do some painting to help pass the time?"

She gave him a grateful look. "Thank you, Your Highness," and then, worriedly, "But... how many days?" If she didn't show up to school on time, they'd give her place to someone else, and it wasn't as if she could call anyone from here and inform them of her delay.

Cole gave a careless wave of his hand. "It doesn't matter. You can go back to any time you choose—as long as it is within your natural life span, of course."

"So, I can't go back and see the dinosaurs?" she teased and was perturbed to see Cole's face darken.

"No," he said shortly. "You wouldn't want to go back then. It was a terrible time for fae."

She let this comment slide, but she couldn't help but think of Bruno. If she could go back to the instant before Bruno died, she could push him out of the way or something. She loathed the man, of course, but no one deserved a terrible death like the one he'd been given.

"There's a mirror in my room that shows Earth and anywhere else you want. Perhaps you'd like to visit it sometime?"

His voice had taken on a suggestive tone, and Ember shot him an indignant look.

He laughed aloud. "I do believe my cousin has scared you off."

She shook her head. "No, I just ... I shouldn't have kissed you. I'm sorry."

He looked perplexed. "But you wanted to."

"Just because I wanted to, doesn't mean I should."

"But I wanted to. And so, I did."

"That's because you're a fae prince, and I'm just a fragile human," she said, with more than a hint of sarcasm.

"You're much more than that, Ember Bailey," he said, and taking her hands, drew her to her feet.

The blanket and cushions had vanished, the soiled plates gone as if they had never existed. Ember didn't even blink. She must be getting used to this strange place, she thought, as they strolled up the hill and back toward the castle.

Spending time outside under the sunny fae sky had calmed her nerves—that is until Ashe had turned up and left her in no doubt that she still had a good while yet before she could return to her regular life. Once again, she had a longing for clean white sheets and perfect peace, but this time she wasn't afraid to say it. Fae did what they wanted, didn't they? Well, maybe for once, she should too.

"I'd like to rest now," she said to Cole, disinclined to utter the more suggestive, "I want to go to bed" and he nodded and took her hand.

"Then that is what you shall do."

"And ... I think it would be best if I stayed out of your way for a bit. For Lissa's sake."

His head shot up at that and he gave her a piercing look that made her squirm.

"Lissa is my teammate, the captain of the Waves. During the games, my power will run through her veins like fire. We will be closer than family, closer than lovers. We've had a dalliance—a rather enjoyable one, as it happens. But I am the prince, and neither Lissa nor my cousin nor you have any right to take me to task."

His brows drew together in a petulant scowl. The sky darkened and Ember blinked.

"I'm sorry," she said. "I wasn't sure what the ... protocol was."

Cole had turned Bruno to a lump of smoking meat, she reminded herself. He could turn on her at any moment. He was powerful. For a moment, she wondered how much stronger he would be if he won the tournament and could wield Ashe's power as well. The thought was sobering.

The sky lightened again as his face cleared. "Of course you weren't. Who could know about Lissa and me? I don't even think I know myself. We have spent time together, in bed," he added with a wicked smile that made his green eyes sparkle and Ember smiled with relief at seeing his good humour return, "and of course she thinks she might become my queen someday, but they all do. She has lovers, I have lovers. We do as we please. Life is for living, for enjoying, for taking and having."

This idea fascinated Ember. She'd always felt life was for enduring, for struggling, with the occasional bright spot, like getting paid her weekly wage or going out for coffee with friends. But Cole's world was all pleasure, all the time. Her life was at the mercy of others: Bruno, her boss, her acceptance into art school. But Cole directed his own life. He made the world as he wanted it. How would it be to live like that?

"None may judge me, save the Adjudicator," Cole said, his expression becoming serious. "That's his job, but certainly not in games of love."

The castle was cool and dim as they stepped through the outer door, and it fascinated Ember that the gardens through the arched windows still appeared as though doused in twilight. Candles flickered as they walked, and Ember wondered why the castle was almost permanently at dusk even when the world outside had moved on.

"Who is the Adjudicator?" she asked.

"He is ancient. The oldest fae alive. He manages the tournament. He will be the one to imprison Ashe."

Or you, she thought, but she didn't say it.

He walked her through the maze of halls until she recognised the place where the forest grew and called for her servant. Lily appeared, curtseying prettily, and Cole instructed her to take Ember back to her room.

"I'll see you soon. Remember, you have the run of the castle. Anything you want."

He gave Ember a courtly bow and reached for her hand, pressing his lips to the back of her hand, and sending an arrow of heat through her, before striding away.

Ember watched him go for a moment, and then she turned and followed Lily back to her room.

CHAPTER 11

L ily brought a pair of silken pyjamas as soon as Ember mentioned, somewhat embarrassed, that she felt too exposed—*prudish*—sleeping in the nude. A new door had appeared in the wall of her chambers, and Lily showed her through to a bathroom, which Ember was sure had not been there before. Perhaps the fae didn't need to take care of bodily functions? thought Ember. Perhaps this room had appeared just for her.

She stepped under a cool shower with drops as gentle as summer rain and spent some time trying out the rack of lotions and perfumes that covered the fragrance spectrum from floral to woody musk to fresh pine. Clean, refreshed and smelling like a florist's shop, she sank into a bed was just as cool and soft as she remembered.

She fell asleep almost immediately, the strain of the day reflected in dreams of a burning tree beside a column of stone. There was an etching of something carved into the slab, the shadow of the outline flickering and moving under the flames of the tree. She drew closer and closer, the carving almost becoming clear, and then she woke.

It wasn't quite light in her room, and she thought dazedly that it must be well before dawn, but then she remembered that the castle lay in twilight, and it could well be the middle of the night, or late afternoon, it didn't matter. She was rested ... and she was hungry.

The door opened as soon as the thought popped into her head, and Lily entered carrying a tray of ... something delicious, Ember thought, as she sat propped up against her pillows, inspecting her breakfast—a thin pancake drizzled with sweet sauce and fresh fruit on the side, followed by juice and an invigorating bitter chocolate drink.

As Ember ate, she watched Lily move about the room, tying back the curtains to let the sweet air in, fluffing up the cushions on the couches, cutting white roses from the window to arrange in a crystal vase. She was light on her feet, but now and then she gave a funny little skip, before appearing to catch herself and resuming her usual graceful movements. Today's uniform was narrower, more utilitarian than the last, and for the first time, Ember noticed two jutting bulges on Lily's back, as though her shoulder blades were swollen. She couldn't help staring and blushed when Lily turned suddenly and caught her.

"I'm sorry," Ember said. "I didn't mean to be rude."

Lily gave her a surprised look. "It's not my place to judge rudeness or not. There is no offence. I am a servant. It doesn't matter what I think."

Ember was quick to refute that. "You're entitled to your opinion. If I was rude, you can say so. You can tell me. I won't mind."

Lily smiled, but she still looked confused. "Certainly. You're curious about my ..." she rolled her shoulders back and a faint shadow of pain crossed her face. "They cut my wings for disobedience. It's ... difficult to get used to."

Ember stopped eating, the thin pancake a mashed-up ball of dough in her mouth that she found hard to swallow. "You had wings?"

She remembered the magnificent trailing wings of those she had seen in the corridors and in the ballroom, the height and width of them, the strength, and then she recalled Lily's funny little skips, as if she were about to take flight—and had suddenly remembered she couldn't.

Lily's eyes grew glossy, and she turned away. Ember didn't like to ask any more questions. Someone had mutilated and brutalised her for doing something wrong, and she clearly didn't want to talk about it. She wondered what Lily had done, who would have done that to her.

"I'm sorry," she said, and set the tray aside, the food only half eaten. She'd lost her appetite.

She went to wash, spritzed herself with some perfume, and returned to find that Lily had laid out a new outfit for Ember to wear. This one was a deep peacock blue, with a scooped neckline and Arabian-style pants that flowed over the hips and tied at the ankle, and a pair of soft blue slippers to match. Lily helped to tie it at the back, and once again, fussed with Ember's hair and tweaked at her clothes until all was to her satisfaction. Without a mirror, Ember couldn't tell, but she *felt* pretty.

"The prince said I might explore the castle," she told Lily. "Will you help me find the forest?"

"Of course," Lily said, and it wasn't long before they were passing under the forest archway.

It was lighter here than in the twilight castle, a peaceful, soft light that recalled early mornings and summer showers. The leafy canopy soared over Ember's head, and she caught the flutter of bright feathers in a tree—a parrot of some sort. It was a dense greenery she'd never experienced before, and it reminded her of tropical forests she'd seen in pictures.

She took off her shoes and left them at the base of a tree, not wanting them to get moss or dirt stained. "I think I'll just hang around here for a bit," she told Lily. "Don't worry about me. You can go, if you like."

Lily gave a little curtsey, telling her that a guide would show her the way back, and left Ember alone to wander the twisting paths. She crushed a handful of scented leaves in her palm, inhaling the sweet fragrance with delight, and picked a red star-shaped flower, tucking it in her hair.

A group of fairies darted around a cluster of white roses, and she paused to watch them, fascinated by their perfect tiny faces, so serious and intent, and their iridescent dragonfly wings. She wandered down more paths, and eventually came to the columns of stone she'd glimpsed earlier.

The columns were arranged as if they were the five points of a star, and looked as though they'd been standing a long, long time. Parts of the lichen-covered stone had crumbled along the edges, and one of them had completely collapsed into a pile of rubble. Each complete column had a symbol etched into the surface—the three drops of water and curling fern frond she'd seen earlier, a jagged peak, and a pair of wings. A complicated mosaic of many-coloured tiles filled the space between them, and creeper plants poked up from the cracks.

She stared at them for a long time. They intrigued her. She wondered what had happened to the collapsed column. They were inside the castle; it was hardly likely to have been knocked down in a storm. Or perhaps it had—she couldn't exactly claim to be an expert on fae meteorology.

Eventually, she left the columns and wandered on, finding herself beside the still pool of water that reflected the painted sky. She sank down next to it, catching sight of her reflection on the surface. She looked ... different, as if a clever make-up artist had enhanced all her features. Her eyes were bigger, her cheekbones more defined, her lips plump. And her hair, usually an unruly mass—the curse of a curly girlie—now coiled obediently about her head, falling past her shoulders in shiny waves. Perhaps it was just the water, she thought, and dabbled her fingers against the surface. Her reflection broke up into ripples, and then she drew back in fright as something pushed its way up out of the water, sending water everywhere.

CHAPTER 12

*C*rocodile! was Ember's first alarmed thought as a scaly head broke the surface, and she scrabbled back from the bank, ready to run. However, it wasn't a crocodile, or any kind of creature at all, but an older woman in a long green dress, her silver hair twisted into a smooth chignon and fixed with sparkling emerald pins, stepping lightly out of the water onto the mossy bank of the pond. She gave herself a shake like a dog, and water flew in all directions, but when she was done, she was perfectly dry.

She greeted Ember with a warm smile, her eyes a startling blue. "Good morning, my dear," although twilight was everywhere, and it could have been high noon or midnight—how did she know? "My name is Alena."

"Hello. I'm Ember. I hope I wasn't intruding. It's so nice here."

"It's by far the finest place in the castle to think," said Alena. "Although the fae haven't discovered that particular pleasure yet. When they do, look out! They'll all be in here, thinking, thinking, thinking, wringing as much joy from it as they can."

"They do like to enjoy themselves," Ember agreed.

Alena regarded Ember closely. "I haven't seen anyone with human in them for years. Forgive me for staring. You have a certain fragile quality. It's very appealing. It makes one want to break you just to see what would happen. Would you shatter like a porcelain plate?"

Ember wasn't sure she quite liked this line of questioning. "No. If I died, I'd just stop and never move again. I wouldn't break into bits or anything."

"Curious," said Alena, pulling up her skirts and settling on the grass next to Ember, a surprisingly limber move for such an elderly person. "When fae vanish from this plane, our energy dissipates into the universe to be used by others. It's all very elegant."

"I suppose that's like us too," said Ember, wondering how to get off this macabre topic before Alena suddenly got ideas. Like Cole, she didn't appear to be very *safe*. Ember didn't want to be her porcelain plate. "We decompose when we die, and our bodies feed the soil and the ... worms and things." *Gross.* "Some people think our souls go to heaven. Other people think our souls are reborn again. And others think nothing happens, that we just wink out and are gone. Nobody knows for sure."

"Somebody knows," said Alena. "They're just not telling the rest of you. Which means it's probably something ghastly. Poor little humans."

There was silence as Ember cast around desperately for something else to say. "It's so beautiful here. I'd like to paint it."

Alena pointed. There behind her, a fae in a uniform similar to Lily's was just setting up an easel with a stool and a table covered with paints and brushes, cloths, and tools. Ember's eyes widened in pleased surprise.

"Thank you!" she called to the servant, who jerked back, startled, and abruptly vanished between the trees. "I think I might try to paint the columns. I think they're fascinating."

"Well, you would," Alena said. "A link to one's past is always fascinating."

Ember frowned. "What do you mean?"

"Come," said Alena, and smoothly rose to her feet. "Leave that," she added, as Ember moved toward the easel, intending to take it with them. "Someone will bring it." And, when they walked through the forest and came to the area where the columns stood, it didn't altogether surprise Ember to see her easel already set up, the rest of the art equipment alongside.

"These are the kingdoms of Esha," Alena said, motioning to each column with a wave of her hand. "Skies, represented by wings, Seeds, with the fern frond, Stones, the mountain peak, Sands, with their drops of precious water." She pointed to the heap of rubble. "And of course, the Shields. Destroyed in a civil war long ago, instigated by ..." she waved an all-encompassing hand to take in the forest and the castle, "... the Swords."

Ember gazed at the columns with fresh respect. The monuments seemed taller and more majestic now that she knew what they stood for.

"You'll see the rulers of all the kingdoms at the tournament," said Alena. "They'll all want to play with you. Be careful, little dolly."

Ember frowned at that, and Alena laughed.

"Why do only the Swords have a tournament?"

"Because the Swords wield greater power than any of the others and must be kept in check. Only one may rule and the other must be confined. When the Shields lost the war, all the kingdoms knew what jeopardy they faced if the Swords were allowed to run unchecked." After a pause, she added, "The tournament has become a tradition, an event of pomp and ceremony, feasts and celebration. The ordinary fae seem to have forgotten that it's a matter of survival. The tournament keeps the Swords in balance. It would be a disaster for all of Esha if anything were to disturb that."

Ember nodded, and Alena smiled and chucked her under the chin as if she were a mischievous little kitten. "I enjoy talking with you. Everyone else thinks they know everything, and only you fully admit you know nothing."

And with that, she *dissolved*, was the only way Ember could describe it, as if she were a puddle of rain drying in the sun, the molecules of her becoming transparent and gaseous, and then vanishing altogether. Ember stared at the space where Alena had been for a full minute, and then, shaking her head in wonder, moved to the easel, and inspected the paints.

She lost herself in her work for a long stretch of time, but because of the unchanging light, had no idea how long she'd been there. Certainly many hours, she thought, when she eventually came back to herself, wincing at the stiffness in her shoulders and neck. She'd only been able to paint at home in snatches when Bruno was out of the house. He thought of her painting as stupid and frivolous, although he certainly didn't mind spending the money when she sold a piece online.

In her painting, the weathered columns of the present had transformed into foreboding edifices, cleared of lichen and aged marks. Instead of rubble, she had brought the column of the Kingdom of Shields back to life, repairing the broken stones and placing it where it would have stood when it was first built. She wasn't sure what the Shields symbol would have been; there was no clue on the fallen stones, and so she improvised, etching a shadowed shield with a glossy pine tree in the centre. She wasn't sure what had inspired a pine in this leafy tropical jungle, but it felt right to her.

She added another brushstroke and then, unsure if the canvas would be tidied away with all her painting equipment, tucked it out of sight behind the fallen stones to work on later.

Leaving the easel, she returned through the forest, found her shoes and slipped them on. Her stomach rumbled, and she thought back to the crepe pancakes that she hadn't eaten that morning with a wistful longing. She was just wondering if she should call out for a servant to show her where to go, when a little golden light zipped through the trees and came to a stop in front of her, hovering in the air. She tentatively reached out to touch it, wondering as she did so if that was the wisest thing to do—it might zap her with a bolt of electricity or something—but it darted back out of her reach and hovered again, plainly waiting for something.

"Could you show me to my room?" she said finally, and the little light bobbed up and down as if happy she had finally made a decision. It moved off between the trees and she followed it out into the hallways.

She had become accustomed to seeing the castle crowded with fae all carefully avoiding her eye, and it was disconcerting to find that the hall was empty. Her footsteps echoed in the silence, and then came a strange sound, a regular pulsing beat that made her spin, looking for the source. It turned out to be coming from overhead; a young fae flying up the hall, the percussion of air moving through his silver tipped feathers, amplified by the soaring ceiling, stone floors, and empty panelled walls. The fae must have seen her, but he didn't acknowledge her and soon rounded a corner, leaving her alone again.

She followed the glowing guide without further incident, and it zipped away as soon as she opened the door to her room. Lily was waiting for her, a tray of food on a low table by the window. Ember headed immediately for the food, but the maid took one horrified glance at her, and insisted she have a shower first to clean the paint off her hands and arms.

The shower was refreshing, and she was positively famished by the time she was done. When she emerged, Lily showed her a shimmering pink dress laid out on the bed, with a set of lacy underwear to match and a pair of pink high heels. There was a velvet box too, and when she opened it, she found a gorgeous necklace cast from hundreds of little gold links, interspersed with sparkling diamonds. With it was a handwritten note:

Dearest Ember, please join me this evening for dinner.
Cole.

CHAPTER 13

E mber's stomach fluttered with nerves as she followed Lily through the castle. The mere suggestion of spending an intimate evening alone with Cole had been enough to make her palms damp. Even though he had explained that his and Lissa's affair was a mere casual liaison, she still felt as though she were encroaching on the other woman's domain. Ember had always had a hard and fast rule to support the sisterhood, but ... did a *water sprite* count?

The layout of the castle was confusing. It was hopeless trying to figure out where she was. The hallways all looked the same, although in this part of the castle, other fae hurried about on their business.

She tagged after Lily, gazing at those strange lumps protruding from her back with a deep sense of sorrow. It must have been terrible to be abused so. Bruno had left bruises, but the thought of him amputating a part of her made her feel sick to her stomach.

She noticed that the fae they passed not only averted their eyes from her but also from Lily, as though Lily's disgrace might be contagious, and she noticed too, that Lily walked with her back straight as if to show that she didn't care what she thought. Her pace was careful and regular, without any sign of the little skips that betrayed her want to fly and join the others swishing over their heads.

Eventually they passed under an archway and drew to a stop in front of two immense doors flanked by guards, who bowed and ushered them in.

Ember, who had been expecting to be shown into a small sitting room with a table for two, hovered in the doorway, taken aback at the sight of a large glittering hall with twisted golden trees lining the walls. A vast table marched down the centre, enough for a hundred seats. All the seats were taken, and every person there was staring at her.

She gave a quick terrified glance at Lily, who merely made a point of raising her chin. Be brave, her look said.

Ember took the hint, and, taking a deep breath, walked forward. Lily followed behind and made her way to the edge of the room, where other fae servants were standing, ready to serve.

"Ember!" A voice came, as soft and intimate as if the two of them were alone together, and Cole appeared in front of her, smiling. "You look enchanting. The necklace suits you."

"Thank you. I love it."

He smiled at that and kissed the back of her hand, before leading her to a seat halfway down the table. She settled in her place and took in her surroundings, the white table linen trimmed in gold, gold candle holders, gold-rimmed wine glasses, golden tulips in crystal vases. The entire effect was ridiculously opulent, almost garish, and it dazzled her.

"This is my team," Cole said, settling into a seat next to her, not at the head of the table, as Ember had thought he might. He indicated with a golden fork as he spoke, "Broude is the head of the Flying Eagles."

Broude was a tall, muscular fae with what Ember was beginning to think of as 'the fae look'; high cheekbones, full lips, pointed ears and an unearthly glowing lustre to the skin. He sat on a stool instead of a high-backed chair, to best accommodate magnificent wings shot with sunset colours of pink, gold and orange.

He nodded at Ember unsmiling, and she nodded back. Cole pointed to another teammate, standing at the table a few seats down, for he was a centaur and had no use for chairs at all. "Swirl."

Swirl looked up as he heard his name and gave Ember an assessing once over before turning back to his conversation. The smile fell from Ember's face at the snub. But then, she thought, maybe all centaurs were like that, aloof and proud, with little use for humans.

"And of course, you know Lissa," Cole finished.

The beautiful water sprite was sitting opposite. She gave Ember a bright smile and Ember smiled tentatively back, wondering if that was the end of their initial mutual animosity. After all, if Cole was telling the truth and Lissa had just been a fling, then Lissa had no real reason to dislike Ember. Besides, Ember was human, and probably the least important one in the room. Definitely the least interesting, she thought, eyeing Broude's wings with a certain covetous air. They were the most beautiful things she'd ever seen. Again, she wondered what Lily's wings had looked like and again felt a deep pain for the girl.

"Ashe's team is down there." Cole gestured toward several others at the far end who were sending unfriendly looks down the table toward him. "I won't introduce you. They're all savages, really."

Ashe was among them, dressed in the dark military style uniform she'd seen him in earlier, but he didn't take any notice of her; his team was his sole focus. In contrast to the opulence of the room, and of the brightly dressed fae around him, he appeared sombre, grave, the dark shadow to their sunshine.

Ember leaned toward Cole and murmured, "And who is that at the end?"

She had seen him as soon as she'd entered the room, and after one glance, she'd looked away, not wanting to attract his attention. If Ashe was daunting, this ... creature ... was positively frightening. He was an older man, cowled and hooded in dark red robes. But it was his eyes that alarmed Ember the most. They looked much older than he was, with crepey lids and red pupils peering out from clouded irises. They were eyes that had seen too much pain and had enjoyed every moment. Behind him stood several other fae, also dressed in dark red, silent and foreboding.

Cole lowered his voice too, and an expression came over his face, one she'd never seen on Cole before, one of almost fearful respect. "That's the Adjudicator and his jury. Do yourself a favour, would you, Ember? Stay out of his way."

If even Cole was fearful of this fae, then now Ember was terrified. She scraped her chair back a little so that the pretty female fae next to her blocked the Adjudicator's view and was careful not to turn in his direction at all, although she could feel his gaze occasionally pass over her, like an icy breeze through a broken window.

Silent servants poured wine and served tiny tasting meals in little bowls. Soft music played through the air. Every so often, a couple would leave the table and dance together, careless of anyone watching as they kissed and caressed, sending a hot flush to Ember's cheeks. One of the male fae had unfastened his partner's silky blouse and was stroking her bare breasts, making her sigh with a cat-like satisfaction. When the song finished, they returned to the table, she casually buttoning her top as if nothing untoward had happened, him with a dangerous glint in his eye that promised something untoward was definitely going to happen after dinner.

Cole noticed Ember watching, and she jumped as he slid a hand on her knee under the table. "Are you enjoying your meal?"

"Y-yes," she replied, with a catch to her breath, as his hand found the side split in her dress and touched her bare skin. A delicious shiver worked through her as his hand slowly drifted up her leg and around to the tender inner thigh. He smiled at her, his darkening gaze focused on her lips, and gave a little growl of satisfaction, as if he knew exactly how much she liked his touch. His fingers trailed higher, and she couldn't help opening her legs a little, welcoming him, and wondering what she would do if he unbuttoned her shirt like the other fae had done earlier, caressed her breasts in front of everyone, leaned over to kiss her nipples...

"You'd better be careful, Your Highness," came a familiar smooth voice, interrupting Ember's fevered train of thought, killing it dead. "You wouldn't want to break your little toy."

Ember's hackles rose at that and she fixed Lissa with a hard look. "I'm tougher than I look."

Cole gave a delighted chuckle, and he squeezed her knee in approval before his hand slid away altogether, leaving Ember feeling strangely cold.

Lissa held up her wineglass in a mock toast and said, "I hear rumours Dansa has been making overtures to the scyllas. What are the rules on bribery?"

Cole shrugged. "None. Dansa may promise what he wishes. It's the follow-through he may find difficult, if he's dead."

He and Lissa turned to look up the table toward Ashe's team, and one of them, a lithe fae with a greenish hue, turned and smiled, showing off pointed teeth.

"Ugh," said Lissa. "He's so obvious."

What was obvious to her was much less so to Ember, and she sat quietly as the talk turned to tactics and strategy. To her surprise, the centaur, Swirl, after his initial aloof dismissal of her, turned out to be rather nice, and explained a few of the rules of the tournament to her.

"Some of it is like a type of relay, run on time. The losing team of each game has their time count against them in the next. It becomes harder and harder for the losing team to catch up, which gives a clear winner, you see?"

"Some of it is like a relay? What's the other part?"

"A fight to the death," said Swirl.

Ember gave him an assessing glance to check if he was joking, but his face was serious. "And if there are three games - air, water and earth, then I'm guessing you're ..."

She was about to say earth, but Swirl nodded gravely. "Air. Yes, I am as light as a feather, with a brain to match." He cast a sideways look at Broude, who had been too busy tearing apart the meat on his plate to pay much attention.

"Huh?" Broude said, when he finally noticed Swirl smirking at him, making those nearby burst into delighted laughter.

As if their levity had alerted the Adjudicator, he rose to his feet. The music stilled and everyone in the room went quiet. Servants backed away from the table and arranged themselves along the wall, their foreheads pressed to the wooden panels as though they weren't even worthy of looking at him. Belatedly, Ember replaced her fork on her plate and the chime of metal resonated in the silence.

The Adjudicator's voice was a scratchy whisper, a desert wind through bones bleached white, and yet Ember didn't have to strain to hear him. His voice was everywhere, resonating through the hall.

"The tournament is a reminder of the tragedy that can befall any of the kingdoms when the balance of power becomes corrupt and ungovernable. Let the fate of the Shields serve as a warning. The penance of containment shall forever be the legacy of the Swords. The games shall decide."

His voice trailed away. There wasn't a sound to be heard, as if everyone at the table was holding their breath, and then he announced, "Lives are sacrosanct until the tournament - here and on Earth."

He gave Ashe and Cole a hard look. Ashe looked blandly back, as if he were completely unaware of the Adjudicator's meaning, while Cole looked as though he was suppressing a smile.

"The tournament will commence in two months."

As if released by the wave of a magic hand, everyone broke into spontaneous chatter. The Adjudicator swept out of the room, followed by the seven jurors without even a farewell; his part in the dinner was done. The servants resumed serving. Some left their seats to converse with friends, others moved to the floor to dance. And then the doors opened and more fae poured in, light and giddy, and ready for fun. Cole moved off into the crowd to dance, surrounded by a group of laughing fae, while Ashe strode off in the opposite direction with his centaur teammate, engrossed in conversation.

The wine flowed freely with toast upon toast offered and drank, and the music became louder, wilder. Circles of flying fae whirled overhead in some complicated dance, and those in the corners kissed passionately, their bodies entwined. And through it all, Ember sat alone at the table, a gnawing in her gut. Two *months?* And then another... however many days for the tournament to run, and then the conclusion of it all. Although Cole had said she could return at any time, she fretted at the delay. Her hair would be longer when she got back, she thought irrelevantly. She'd only just got it cut.

Suddenly fed up, she caught Lily's eye and rose to her feet, ready to head back to her room to sleep, when a firm hand gripped her wrist, biting into her flesh.

"Where do you think you're going?"

CHAPTER 14

E mber jerked her hand away from Lissa, the small bones in her wrist tender. The water sprite was taller than Ember and she took advantage of her height, looming over Ember in a threatening manner. Far from feeling threatened, Ember felt cross. She'd put up with enough of that from Bruno and look where he was now. She straightened her back, lifted her chin.

"I'm going to bed," she said, and, because her wrist still hurt where Lissa had grabbed her, cast a glance toward Cole, letting a slow smile crease her lips. *With Cole* was the unspoken taunt.

Lissa took the bait, snapping, "Keep your filthy human hands to yourself. Cole and I are ..."

"Are what?" Ember said. "He told me you two were just having fun."

On anyone else, a red angry flush would have made them appear uncomfortably hot, but on Lissa, the faint flush colouring her cheeks looked enchanting.

"Cole will need someone by his side when he rules, and that some-one is me. We have an understanding."

Her eyes shone with conviction, her proud head held high, and a wave of shame came over Ember. What was she doing, being unkind to a woman, a sprite, whatever, who was in love?

"You needn't worry about me," Ember said. Lissa gave a growl deep in her throat and Ember realised she'd sounded as if Lissa definitely had something to worry about. She hastened to explain, "I won't be here long. Once the tournament is done, I'll be gone too."

"Just stay out of his way," Lissa said, slowly and deliberately, as though Ember was a small child who could only understand small words.

"And how am I supposed to do that?" Ember said, exasperated. "It's his castle. I can't go anywhere else. Even the clothes I'm wearing are his. I can't refuse him."

Lissa's eyes flickered over the necklace Ember wore. "No. You can't. But I don't have to like it."

She slid off into the crowd and Ember, sorely tempted to throw up her hands in disgust, stomped off toward the door with Lily in tow.

But before she'd made it five strides, Broude stopped her. He made her a courteous bow and held his hand out to her to dance. She hesitated a moment and then smiled in acquiescence. After all, how often would she have a chance to dance with a real-life fairy? With an apologetic shrug to Lily, she took his hand.

She didn't know the steps, but it was a whirling, haphazard dance that had Broude twirling her under the canopy of his wings, her feet skipping, one way and then the other, until she was giddy and breathless. Every now and then, he would spread his wings and lift her gently off the floor. The first time he'd done it, she clung to him in fright, not knowing how high he was going to go and wondering if he had a strong enough grip to prevent her falling, but she soon got used to it, enjoying the feeling of weightlessness in his strong arms.

When the music finally died, she gave him a bright, pleased smile, thanking him and he bowed again, formally, and left her.

She was looking around for Lily, when a hand slid around her waist and gathered her in - Cole, with an irresistible twinkle in his eye. "I saw you dancing. I'm glad you're enjoying yourself."

At once, the energetic music slowed, the beat becoming slow and seductive, the melody romantic and sweet. Ember gave him a suspicious look, and he laughed, one hand taking hers and placing it on his shoulder in a classic waltz position. "Come now, you can't deny that you're just a little weary after dancing with Broude. He's an athlete. He expects everyone to keep pace with him."

"Well," admitted Ember, "He was fairly ... energetic."

Cole smiled at her, drawing her close. "Sometimes one has to read the situation and then act accordingly." His breath tickled her ear, and she drew in a deep breath, not wanting her body to betray her with those telltale shivers, but there they were, coursing through her veins, making her blood thrum. For an instant, she closed her eyes, feeling the heat between their bodies, but when she opened her eyes again, she saw Lissa glaring at her from the other side of the room.

Ember gave herself a mental shake and pushed back from Cole a little. "I think you're holding me a little close," she said, and Cole's eyes darkened.

"So?"

"So, I don't think it's such a good idea."

"Why?"

Good question. "Because … because I'm a human and I don't belong here, and everyone knows it. And because I don't want to upset anyone."

She'd become accustomed to Cole's easy-going manner, and she didn't expect his cold response. "You needn't worry about upsetting anyone else. Your concern should be with upsetting *me*. I am the prince. I am *your* prince." His eyes had become feral, the hand on her waist a block of iron. She drew back, alarmed. He looked as though he was about to snarl at her, his teeth sharp enough to rip her throat out.

"I'm sorry," she stammered. "I didn't mean to offend you. I just don't want to cause any trouble."

As if the sun had come out from behind a cloud, the shadow lifted from Cole's face, his features back to their usual charming state, his manner debonair and courteous. "You're no trouble. No trouble at all."

His ill temper had been so fleeting she wondered if she had imagined it, and after a moment's hesitation, she came to him again. As they dipped and twirled around the room, Ember became conscious that others were watching, and this time, they weren't muttering behind their hands and side-eyeing her. They were watching with approval, with envy, with fascination. Under their gaze, and in the arms of the most handsome, most desirable fae in the room, she felt beautiful, dazzling. She couldn't help a pleased smile curve her lips, couldn't help the inviting sway of her hips. She couldn't see Lissa anywhere anymore, and she was glad for that. But there was also a disquiet within her too, as she obediently followed Cole's lead. Like a doll, she realised. Like a toy brought out to play.

The music ended, and she gave Cole a curtsey as he claimed the back of her hand in a kiss. When he turned away to talk to someone else, she seized the moment and took off in the other direction, pushing through the crowd, not wanting to even find Lily in case someone waylaid her again.

"I can ask for a guide," she thought as she slipped into the hallway. "The light will help me back to my room."

She darted into an alcove, hands folded together in a classic prayer position as she wished fervently for a guide, when she heard a voice.

"Are you lost?"

She opened her eyes, wondering if the glowing ball of light had perhaps become articulate, and then she gasped, her hand flying to her mouth in surprise.

Ashe.

CHAPTER 15

E mber didn't know what to say. Ashe was the antithesis to Cole. The two princes were both devastatingly handsome, albeit in an alien way, exuding power and control. But while Cole gave off an aura of fun and merriment, of careless pleasure and light-hearted play, Ashe appeared as though he carried the universe on his broad shoulders and hated every moment. Even now, speaking innocuously to her, his heavy brows were lowered, his mouth grim, as though he'd rather set her on fire than speak to her.

"I was just waiting for a guide back to my room," she said, and added, "I hope it's not you."

She regretted it as soon as she had said it. What on earth did she say that for? How rude! What she'd meant was, she hoped he wouldn't waste his time on a servant's task, but it had come out utterly, utterly wrong. She peeped up at him, cheeks hot with embarrassment, half expecting to see a furious scowl. But to her relief, he didn't look angry—well, no angrier than usual. In fact, he didn't even look as though he had heard her. He was scanning the candlelit hall, left, right, and overhead, hand on his sword hilt.

"You should stay in your room," he said. "It's dangerous for you out here. There are too many rivalries, too many opportunities for you to get hurt. You're ... more fragile than the rest of us."

"The Adjudicator said that lives are sacrosanct," she reminded him. "I assumed that meant mine as well."

"Accidents happen."

The loaded way he said it sent a chill down Ember's back. Quick as thought, he reached out and seized her arm, twisting it. She drew a breath to scream, but he wasn't trying to hurt her, merely inspecting a paint smudge on the back of her upper arm that she'd failed to remove earlier. "What's that?"

"Just paint," she said, tugging her arm free. "I was painting in the forest today."

He blinked, and a slow smile curved his mouth. It was disconcerting to see him like that, smiling. It changed his entire face, made him look almost ... no. He definitely did not look friendly. "Creating something out of nothing? How human." He didn't sound patronising, rather, surprised and appreciative, and he hastened to explain. "We—fae—cannot create as such. We can replicate and elaborate on what is already there, but we cannot make something original from nothing."

"Oh. I didn't know that. That's ... sad."

All those marvels she had seen around the castle, all copied from the human world? Nothing innovative, nothing created from a leap of intuition, hard work, accident, or luck. What would she do if she couldn't paint? That gnawing itch when an idea unbidden crawled its way into her skull, the leap of joy when the ephemeral was transferred to canvas and made tangible. How frustrating, to have an idea that could never be completed.

"It wouldn't occur to any of the fae to try," he explained, as if he knew the direction of Ember's thoughts. "They're—we're—not missing out."

For a moment, she felt almost sorry for the fae having their powers curtailed, limited by a lack of creativity. On impulse she said, "Would you like to see my painting?"

He looked surprised. "I cannot go into Cole's area of the castle. Only the common areas."

"The forest is a common area though, isn't it?" She remembered Lily saying so as they passed under the huge carved archway.

He considered this, his habitual frown creasing his forehead, and nodded. "Then it seems as if I am your guide, after all."

He moved off down the corridor, not the way she'd come, but in the opposite direction, and she hesitated, wondering what on earth she'd let herself in for, before trotting after him. They walked in silence, a circuitous route that took them down wood panelled hallways, along a gallery lined with colourful statues, and through huge, gilded rooms that looked out over the twilight gardens. The forest was further than she'd imagined, and she wished she could invite him into Cole's area, if only to shorten the distance. She took off her high heels and although he eyed them dangling from her fingers, he made no comment.

She continued walking a half pace behind him, noting the way other fae scurried out of his way pretending not to notice him, and she realised that when they'd been doing it to her it wasn't, as she'd initially thought, out of discourtesy or aloofness but as a sign of respect. She wondered uneasily if Cole would know she'd gone and what he would think if he knew she was here with his greatest rival. The thought was unnerving. She'd seen a glimpse of Cole's temper, and she didn't much like it.

On the other hand, this might be a good time to beg Ashe if he could use some of his powers to send her home. If the tournament didn't begin for another two months, perhaps he had time to recharge himself? Like a battery, she supposed with amusement, imagining Ashe plugging himself into a socket in the wall and lighting up like a Christmas tree. But he'd already said no, and she didn't want to nag him and perhaps push him into never letting her go.

Around and around her thoughts went, and she was about to tell Ashe that she was tired and maybe they should see her picture another time, when finally, they were there.

The forest was just as light and loamy as ever, and her worries flew out of her head, heart lifting, as she passed beneath spreading boughs and heard the faint trills of birds flying through the canopy.

"This is my favourite place," she commented happily, and Ashe lifted an eyebrow in confusion, as if he couldn't quite believe that she preferred the dirt of the jungle to the elegance of the great hall.

"I haven't been here since I was small."

She smiled to herself. A little Ashe! All dressed up in a black soldier uniform with a frown creasing his little boy face.

"Have you met Alena yet?" He had lowered his voice to a hush, and she wondered at that. It sounded as though he might be in awe of her.

"Yes. I liked her."

Ashe gave a little shake of his head, as if in disbelief. "She can choose to be likeable," was his cryptic reply.

It was Ember who led the way this time, and when they came to the columns of the kingdoms, he gave a little sigh and rocked back on his heels, hands behind his back, as he gazed at the four towering pillars and the heap of rubble.

"Where is the column for the Kingdom of Swords?"

He gave her a surprised look. "You only see the Sword Column when you're in another kingdom. They all have an area where the columns stand. They're doorways."

"You can use them to get into another kingdom? How do they work?" The columns had been fashioned from smooth stone. There were no seams showing a door that she could see.

"You have to be fae," he told her, and she frowned. Of course.

She retrieved her canvas from behind the rubble where she'd left it and presented it to him, suddenly shy. He looked at it with no hint of any reaction on his face. "You made the Shields whole again."

For an instant she wondered if she'd misinterpreted some other cultural rule she hadn't known about, and when he eventually said, "It's very good," she gave a mock 'whew', wiping a hand over an imaginary sweaty brow and smiling at his obvious puzzlement.

He raised a hand over the canvas, and she gave a cry of delight. It was as though he'd turned the picture into a three-dimensional window. The leaves on the trees moved gently in an invisible breeze and birds flew from branch to branch. Insects darted in and out of the flowers, while the columns themselves glowed with a soft inner light.

"What did you do? That's amazing!"

He looked pleased, but also disconcerted, as though he hadn't expected her delight. "It's just a glamour, a way to manipulate the senses and make you think something is there when it isn't." His eyes flickered over her, pausing at the gold and diamond necklace around her neck, and then up to her face again. "It's a way of controlling someone."

The smile froze on her face. He'd made a simple, pretty trick into something horrible, perverse. She couldn't prevent the emotions passing over her face, and he frowned, waving his hand over the painting again, restoring it back to what it was. She took it back in silence. The painting that she had been so happy with suddenly appeared flat, uninspiring, amateurish. Carefully, she placed it back among the stones; it was still a little tacky and wet in places.

"I think I'd like to go back to my room now."

"Come now, Ember," he said, and she looked up at him in surprise, not used to such gentle tones from someone so habitually terse. "Don't run away when things don't go your way."

She started at that and blinked. "I'm not. I'm just tired."

Although ... perhaps he had a point. She'd chosen to run from Bruno, rather than stand up to him and continue living her own life on her own terms in the town she'd made her own. That wasn't her fault though, she argued with herself. Bruno was a violent abuser, and he would have made her life a misery even if she had thrown him out. She'd never reported him though, had told no one else, not even those she'd thought of as friends. She'd never gone to the police, insisted they help her. She had felt embarrassed, ashamed. Besides, everyone said how difficult it was to get help through official channels, and so she hadn't even bothered to try. Why fight when you can run? Despite that, Ashe's words cut to the very core of her, as though she was in the wrong, and she didn't like it.

He considered her for a moment and then shrugged. "Very well."

He beckoned to somewhere beyond the trees, and a ball of light came zigzagging through the forest toward her. It hesitated as it became aware of Ashe, and then glowed brighter and brighter, growing larger and larger. Ember watched the swelling ball of light in some alarm, but with Ashe's words still ringing in her ears, she didn't take so much as a half step back.

Ashe, however, was smiling with wry amusement. "I think we may be in trouble."

Suddenly, the light exploded in a blazing fountain of sparks, and there stood Cole.

CHAPTER 16

C ole's jaw was set, his eyes hard, and the corner of his mouth flickered, the only physical betrayal of his tension. His blond hair looked almost bleached bone white, a match to the shadowy aura that hung around him, a cloud of smoke, fury made tangible. He didn't so much as glance at Ember, but she still had the urge to cut and run back to her room as fast as she could. The only relief she felt was that his temper wasn't directed at her. Ashe was the sole recipient of his anger.

"She is mine." His voice was deathly calm. "Mine."

As apprehensive as she was, Ember shot him a frown at that. She wasn't anyone's. No one owned her. She was about to open her mouth and refute him, but she held back. He had rescued her from Bruno after all—sort of. And he had given her that gorgeous room and the beautiful clothes, and the gold necklace around her neck. But it wasn't just that which made her hold her tongue. There was a warning glint in Ashe's eye that told her it might not be the best idea if she interrupted Cole while he was in this mood.

"Forgive me, Cousin," Ashe said, lightly. "She was lost."

"You were both lost. Together."

Ashe swept Cole a sarcastic bow. "If it bothers you, then I shall go and get lost by myself."

He turned to Ember and took her fingers, placing a light kiss on the back of her hand. She could feel his lips smiling as he did so. He was enjoying this. She snatched her hand away as soon as he'd released it, resisting the urge to wipe it on her skirts.

He strode off between the trees, a mocking, "See you later," drifting back to them.

Ember dug her toe into the soft earth, finally working up enough courage to look at Cole. To her surprised relief, the anger had left his face, the shadowy aura chased away as if the sun had come out on a cloudy day. He looked contrite, almost sorrowful.

"I'm sorry, Ember," he said. "I was a poor host. I should have taken better care of you. I didn't realise you wanted to leave and I'm sorry you ended up in such vile company."

"Oh ..." Ember said, eager to make things right between them. "No, it was fine. And you were busy. I was just tired, and I didn't want to disturb you. It was a little overwhelming, all the dancing and music and everything."

He came to her and took her hands, looking deep into her eyes. "And you were worried about dancing with me in front of Lissa?"

"She told me you two had an understanding," Ember said. "I don't want to make things awkward."

"Lissa is possessive. But no one tells me what to do." And then he added, half under his breath, "Look what happened to Serafina."

Before she could ask what he meant, he slipped an arm around her waist, pulled her to him, and the thought slid out of her mind.

There was no hesitation before kissing her this time, no unspoken request for permission. His mouth ground down on hers, stealing her breath, making her knees weaken, and she closed her eyes as the world swam around her. There was nothing else but his kiss, nothing but the loosening of her muscles, the heat building within her, the stirring of something dark and delicious. She wound her arms around his neck and gave herself up to him, her tongue exploring his mouth, pressing herself against him, and feeling the hard response of his body in return.

There came a feeling like wind rushing past, and when she opened her eyes again, she was somewhere else. The forest had disappeared. Cole released her, and she staggered, overcome by both the power of her physical arousal and the displacement of time and space.

Trying to regain her senses, she blurted, "where are we?" although it was fairly obvious where they were. This had to be Cole's personal sanctuary. Tones of rich cream and gold were dominant, with a fire crackling in an enormous fireplace and candles lighting dark corners. A mirror stood in one corner showing, not the reflection of the room, but a cityscape by night. The view looked familiar, but she couldn't think what it was for the moment.

Against one wall was a huge four-poster bed, warm with a thick covering of white fur, gauzy curtains pulled back against the posts with golden tasselled cords. A table by the bed had wine chilling in an ice bucket and two glasses, and a bowl of fruits and sweets. Soft music filled the air, not romantic and sweet, but a dark and seductive beat that made her want to raise her arms and gyrate her hips, as though she was out in some nightclub somewhere, drunk and high, and blissfully uncaring.

"This is my room," he said.

She gave a nervous laugh. "I guessed."

He came to her again and kissed her, a kiss that was initially gentle, and then, in quick response to her eager arousal, hard and demanding. He slid his hands up her waist and gently tugged at the narrow ribbons holding the bodice of her dress together. The ribbons loosened, and the bodice parted, exposing her breasts encased in a pink lace bra. He kissed the tops of her breasts, cupping them together, and then suckled at her peaked nipples through the lace.

He kissed her mouth again, and his arms tightened around her, pulling her into him so that she could feel his hot arousal. His hand slipped down, and he touched her between her legs, stroking her through her dress. She moaned against his mouth. There was too much fabric in the way. She wanted his hands and tongue against her bare flesh; she wanted him to taste her.

"Please, stop …" she tore herself from his embrace and moved back, her breathing as fast as if she'd been running. Her heart was hammering in her chest, her thoughts muddied.

His eyes glittered, but he made no move to stop her. It was the calm acceptance of her rejection, that her refusal didn't anger him, that made her carry on.

She lifted trembling hands to the front clasp of her bra, snapping the catch and letting her breasts bounce free. He watched, silent, his face betraying nothing. She shimmied her bra off her shoulders, and then tugged at the waist of her dress until it fell in a glimmering pile at her feet. Lifting her arms, she pulled at the pins holding up her hair, and shook her head, so that her hair tumbled down her back in a wavy river of black. Clad in nothing but a pair of pink lace briefs, she stepped slowly toward him, pressed her body against his, and kissed him.

Quicker than thought, his arm was about her waist, and he had lifted her, propelling her to the bed. His mouth fused to hers, his hands fisted in her hair. She moaned and pushed up, arching her back. He bent his head, claiming her naked breasts, squeezing them with his hands, licking and sucking her nipples until they were hot and aching.

The fur underneath her was soft and caressing, and his body over hers, hard and unyielding. The scent of him was all-encompassing, intoxicating. She couldn't think, she could only feel his hands and mouth exploring her: biting, pinching, stroking, caressing.

He slid further down the bed, nuzzling at her wet heat, and she yanked the sopping lace down so that he could get to her properly. He lapped at her with long, leisurely strokes, and she could feel her muscles clenching convulsively, desperate for a quick release.

He didn't give it to her though, and she almost cried out with disappointment as he moved away from her, the building fire within her suddenly doused.

"Ember." His voice was ragged, and she could see that he was just as aroused as she, perhaps even more so. His pupils had dilated so much that the green was just a thin circle, and his pulse was jerking in his throat. He was naked—although how he had removed his clothing without her noticing, she hadn't the faintest—and his cock was rigid, impressively so. She wanted it. She wanted him.

"I need this," he groaned, and she thought perhaps she had misheard him, that he meant to say, "I need you," and eager to please, she reached for him, opening her legs, guiding him to her.

He rested there for a moment, and she squirmed, the hot tip of him nudging at her. Her muscles clenched again uncontrollably, an unbearable tension rising within her.

"Do it," she begged, and with a groan, he drove into her, burying himself to the hilt.

She came almost at once, and when she did, he gasped, as though he had felt the same explosion of stars as she had. A cloud of mist roiled about them, and dazed, she wondered if their passion had transported them skyward and they were somehow having sex in the clouds.

He switched position, lifting her legs over his shoulders, pulling out to the head, and then diving in deep again. She gasped as new sensations overwhelmed her, the delicious friction building faster than she'd ever thought was possible for her, and within a few strokes, she came again.

Her orgasm made his eyes flutter closed, and he groaned. The mist flickered with a blaze of light, as though lightning in a storm. He brought a hand down to rub her clit and thrust again, and again, fast and deep. She was thrashing, crying out his name. His fingers were relentless, dragging her to the edge again, and as she shattered, he came too, his release a wild cry mingling with hers.

His weight came down on her as he collapsed. He was trembling, his skin heated as though he had a fever, the mist slowly dissipating. With an effort, he rolled away from her, and she gave a tiny mew of disappointment, too satiated and languid to give voice to a complaint. He gave a low chuckle and pressed a kiss to her temple.

"You're on my side, aren't you?" he murmured. "I need you here with me, supporting me."

"Of course," Ember said, drowsily. The fire in the fireplace was warm, comforting, the fur on the bed pliant and soft against her tender skin.

He said something else, but she couldn't hear him clearly. The dark was claiming her now, and she slept.

CHAPTER 17

The mirror shattered and the reflective shards flew past her as if in a strong wind, slicing at her flesh, fire and ice, cutting deep and drawing blood ...

She awoke with a gasp in her own room, and held out her hands, expecting to see bloody lacerations across her palms and wrists, but there was nothing. She ached pleasurably though, deep in the secret parts of her, and a hot flush crawled up her cheeks as she recalled the night before.

"A bath is waiting for you." Lily's soft voice sounded from the shadows of the room, and she padded forward into the light, holding out a silk robe for her.

Ember slid it on and padded into the bathroom to wash. There were bruises, scratches and what looked like bites all over her body, but the water was soothing, and the stinging soon eased. It hadn't been a dream. It was all real. She'd had sex with Cole. More than that, she'd had the best sex of her *life*. He had wrung sensations out of her, drop by scandalous drop, that she hadn't even imagined were inside her. Lissa's face floated into her head, and she forced it out again. Right now, she didn't care what Lissa thought. She liked what Cole had done to her. She wanted more.

Lying in a blissful reverie, she soaped herself lazily, her flesh remembering another touch, another pair of hands, another's fingers ... and then she sat up abruptly, splashing water on the tiled floor. Here she was, fantasising about Cole when she could be having the real thing.

She settled at the table in her robe, and Lily served her a hot breakfast, all Earthly things, Ember noted with surprise and gratification: eggs, bacon, croissants, fried tomatoes and mushrooms, and a pot of strong coffee.

She ate quickly, ravenous, while Lily laid out a choice of clothes. Ember chose a top and matching skirt in soft buttercup yellow with gathered detailing that accentuated the curve of her breasts. Like everything she had worn so far, it felt soft and luxurious, especially against her bruised skin. Lily asked if she wanted a soothing ointment to heal the fiery marks on her body, but Ember refused. In some perverse way, she liked the pain. She wanted a reminder of what Cole had done to her.

"I'm glad you returned safely." Lily tied the ribbons of the skirt at Ember's back, drawing the waist in so that it flared out over her hips, giving her a classic hourglass shape without the discomfort of a corset. "You should be careful roaming the castle hallways, especially at night. It would be best if I accompanied you in the future."

"I'm sorry," said Ember, remembering uneasily that this was the second warning she'd had to be careful in the hallways. "I thought I'd be safe enough. I went to the forest with Ashe, and then Cole found me and ..."

Lily's eyes grew wide, although she was making an obvious effort to school her expression. "Two Princes in one night?" She gave a horrified squeak and covered her mouth. "I'm so sorry ..."

Ember burst out laughing. Lily ducked her head, embarrassed, and then glanced at Ember with a shy smile.

"It's alright," said Ember. "Ashe was just showing me the way, and then Cole turned up and ..."

"I can guess," Lily said dryly, who had deliberately fixed Ember's hair so that it covered the bite marks on her neck. "You don't have to explain, but please be careful. The princes are not to be trifled with. They hold the power of life and death of everyone in the kingdom, and after the tournament ..."

Her voice trailed off, and she busied herself with Ember's ribbons again.

"I understand," said Ember, but she didn't really, and she felt sure of Cole. He wouldn't hurt her. He had told her he needed her as moral support through the tournament, and she believed him. Just the thought of him was enough to bring a delicious melting in her stomach and a heat rising to her cheeks.

Lily turned her around and considered her closely before pronouncing her done. Ember looked down at her skirts, smoothing them with her fingers. "I wish I could see myself. I've only seen one mirror in the castle, and it doesn't even show any reflections."

"A mirror! Of course. I'll have it put in the bathroom. It's there now."

Ember picked up her skirts and ran to the bathroom, hardly able to believe a mirror had just appeared in the time it took them to exchange a few words, but yes, there it was, a large gold-framed mirror on the wall that reflected from head to toe. Ember called out to Lily to thank her, and made a little twirl, admiring the way her dress flared out before settling in all the right places. The soft yellow gave her an innocent virginal air, but the cut was decidedly not, low in front and clinging to her hips, the material of the skirts so sheer it showed her lace underwear underneath. She would never in a million years wear anything like this back home, but here, in this place of passion, luxury and unbridled excess, it seemed entirely appropriate.

Her gaze wandered up to the reflection of her face, her lips still swollen from kisses, her cheeks flushed with pleasure, the marks of Cole's passion on her neck, and then her eyes widened, and her hand flew to her throat. The gold and diamond necklace she wore had changed. She was sure of it. It looked like a leather collar. Just for an instant, and then it had become a sparkling gold and diamond band again. She squinted at it, but it remained the same and she decided her eyes—or the mirror—must have been playing tricks on her.

When she returned to the bedroom, Lily was holding out a wicker basket to her, and she took it in some surprise.

"This just arrived for you." Lily's voice was expressionless, but Ember was too excited at the thought of a present to notice. She opened the basket and out tumbled a roly-poly bundle of white fur, all pink tongue and scrabbly feet with a flicker of diamonds, and she gasped in delight.

"A puppy! Oh, how gorgeous."

She picked the puppy up and it snuggled into her, covering her chin with puppy kisses.

"He'll ruin your hair." Lily was disapproving, and Ember laughed.

"What does that matter? He's lovely!" She admired his pretty white fur and the diamond collar around his neck before setting him down. At once, he ran off to explore. She watched him fondly and took out the note at the bottom of the basket.

'A gift for my greatest treasure. I wear your scent today like perfume. Come and find me at the training grounds - C.'

She gave a small, secret smile. "I have to go to the training grounds. Will you come?"

"Of course," said Lily, bobbing her head. "It does me no good if you're injured or murdered in the hallways."

Ember shot Lily a frown at that, but then the puppy came and licked her toes, making her giggle and reach for her shoes.

"He needs a ... oh thank you," as Lily handed her a leash before she could finish her sentence. She clipped it to the puppy's collar and the three of them left the room.

CHAPTER 18

I t was sunny outside. The grounds were warm and tranquil and there was the delicious scent of lemon blossom in the air. Ember didn't want to let the puppy off the lead in case he ran off, never to be seen again, or to be, as Lily warned her, a meal for the many creatures that stalked the forests outside the castle grounds. Instead, he frolicked and bit at the lead, trying to tug her off course to investigate some exciting fresh smell, barking ridiculous little puppy barks at every bird that flew overhead.

"Don't let him chase the fairies," Lily said, as he bounded over to a clump of flowers surrounded by tiny glowing lights. "They're poisonous."

"Goodness!" said Ember, and hastily picked the puppy up, out of the way. "We can't have that, can we, little Rufus?"

"Rufus?" said Lily.

"I'm just trying it out," Ember said. "Rufus? Gregory? Peter? I quite like pet names that are real names, don't you?"

Lily shrugged. "I've never owned a living creature."

The way she said it, as though the idea of having a pet was offensive or shameful, made Ember feel uncomfortable. As soon as they were clear of the fairy infested flowers, she set the puppy down again and followed Lily in silence.

The two walked along the paths, and for a time, beside a sparkling river flowing easily around large flat stones used for crossing over to the other side. A rumble of rushing water grew louder as they rounded a curve, and they came out onto a flat piece of ground where the river abruptly ended in a large waterfall, the volumes of water crashing down and down, to a series of pools far below. The castle wall was evident just beyond, and further out from that, peaceful meadows, thickets of forest, and a couple of what looked like toy villages.

"The Falls," said Lily, absently, giving the beautiful view a cursory glance as though such sights were commonplace. Spray drifted back up, settling onto their clothes and hair in a fine mist, and Ember longed to take the path leading to the bottom of the waterfall, and set up her easel to paint it.

The path they took instead curved around again and, leaving the waterfall behind, they came to a vast, cleared meadow fenced with white railings. Inside, a team of centaurs thundered around an obstacle course of hills and jumps and wide ponds. Foam flecked their flanks, their chests heaved, and they strained with effort as they leapt across the jumps and galloped down the straights. The brawny creatures must have been training for hours already. Fae lined the fence-line, shouting instructions and encouragement.

Lily scanned the area closely, and then said with an air of grudging approval, "You'll be safe enough. I will leave you for now." She took the leash from Ember's hand. "And I'll take the little one. He might end up mashed under the centaurs' hooves."

Ember laughed. "You seem determined that he's going to come to an awful end. First eaten by wild beasts, then poisoned and now trampled."

Lily gathered the puppy into her arms. "He is very engaging," she allowed, as the puppy, tired after his walk, snuggled in. "I should hate to see him hurt."

"Do you think you could find him a basket to sleep in? And a blanket. And some toys. And food bowls and things."

"Of course," Lily said. "It is done already."

Of course.

"Just call me when it's time to leave," said Lily. "Don't try to find the way on your own."

"Alright."

Lily left with the puppy, and Ember walked toward the spectators. She recognised some of them—Tinth the centaur on Ashe's team, standing with Ashe himself, and, further along the fence, Lissa with Cole. She took a moment to admire Cole's broad shoulders and muscular physique, and the way his clothes draped across his frame, accentuating all the best bits, she thought. As if he could feel her eyes on him, Cole turned, and immediately left Lissa, coming to her and taking her into his arms.

"I missed you," he said simply, before kissing her. She clung to him, the sound of the centaurs' hooves thrumming in her ears along with the beat of her heart, hard and fast. She wanted him. Just one kiss was all it took and all she could think about was his room and that bed and him doing things to her that made her pant and writhe.

He broke the kiss, leaving her blinking, and as she regained her senses, tucked her hand into the crook of his elbow and walked her over to the fence.

"Our first open training," said Cole, indicating Ashe and Tinth nearby. "There's a fine line between showing the other team how formidable we are without giving away all our secrets. Fortunately, Swirl is more than capable of dealing with scrutiny."

Lissa was eyeing Ember with open hostility, but as Ember and Cole approached, she forced a friendly smile. It was costing the other woman though; there was a faint tremble to her hands and when she said airily to Ember, "How now, little one? Have you come to cheer on our team?" she sounded as if she was chewing on broken glass.

Ember appreciated the gesture, although she didn't much like being called 'little one' as though she were a child. "Good morning, Lissa. Yes, I like to be on the winning side."

This earned her a pleased squeeze of the hand and a light kiss brushing her temple, and she closed her eyes, wishing it were just the two of them and everyone else was far, far away.

Cole dropped her hand and said, "I must see Swirl," and when he left her side, she felt it as a physical thing, as though someone had severed a part of her from herself. She watched him go, anxiety crawling through her, unable to take her eyes from him, and was hardly aware when Ashe approached until he was right next to her.

"Good morning, Lissa. Are you guarding the human?"

"Hardly," said Lissa, with a snort. "If you want to turn her to dust, be my guest."

This caught Ember's attention, and she scowled.

Ashe laughed. "It wouldn't take much."

Ember felt his eyes on her, raking her neck. Her hair had blown back over her shoulder, and she knew the bruises were starkly visible on her skin.

"You should ask your maid for some ointment for that," Ashe said. "An infection may start."

"Humans are too fragile for fae," said Lissa. "It must be like making love to a pastry. One bite and it collapses."

"Only fae can satisfy fae," agreed Ashe.

Ember could feel her temper rising. "Well, perhaps you should get a move on and send me back. We're all just waiting on you."

Ashe looked at her in surprise, and Lissa let out a delighted gasp. "How *can* you speak to the prince so? Your Highness, she must be punished. If you need to present a credible witness to her audacity and lack of grace, I shall do so gladly."

Ember gritted her teeth, forcing her hands to remain at her sides before she slapped Lissa with all her strength. She glared at Ashe with her eyebrow raised as if daring him, and when he made no move, no comment at all, she gave them both a cross curtsey. It was a bit of a clumsy one and Lissa sniggered, but Ashe remained silent, and Ember turned on her heel and walked off, fuming.

CHAPTER 19

E mber stomped along the path back toward the waterfall, too cross to bother calling Lily to escort her back. Part of her wanted to stay and watch Cole regardless of the others, but there was another part of her that just wanted to be on her own, away from barbed comments and veiled looks. She should just spend the rest of her time in her room, she thought resentfully. A few days confined with everything at her beck and call wouldn't be so bad, would it? But then she thought of Cole and how he had told her he needed her, and her heart melted. She couldn't just leave him when he was about to go into the tournament. He needed her there, watching and supporting from the sidelines.

As she approached the bend in the path by the waterfall, mists rose to greet her, cool and calming against her skin. And when she turned the corner and beheld the vista of water plunging down the falls into the valley below, the cool blue pools churning with white froth, and the gentle rise and fall of the surrounding hills, she could hardly believe that it was all real. It looked too perfect, like a movie set. Apart from one thing, way off in the distance, a stain of brown amongst the green rolling hills. She squinted, trying to make it out. It looked like a broken city skyline, just the jagged tops showing above the trees, but it was so far away, she couldn't be sure. Perhaps it was just scrub-free hills, but she wasn't sure about that either.

There came the sound of light footsteps and she turned, letting out a sigh of irritation when she saw Lissa was the source, golden hair gleaming in the sun, her pink skirts billowing around her like candy floss.

"What?" she said disagreeably, as Lissa drew to a halt in front of her.

"Don't be like that," Lissa said tartly. "It wasn't my idea to be here. His Highness told me to escort you back to the Palace. Believe me, I've got better things to do."

"Perhaps you should go and do them then," said Ember, fully aware that she sounded like a petulant child, but unable to stop herself.

Lissa rolled her eyes. "And disobey the prince? Not likely."

Ember took another look at the brown stain on the horizon and pointed. "What's that way over there?"

"What's left of the Kingdom of Shields," Lissa said, shortly.

Ember's eyes widened. When she'd heard that the kingdom had been destroyed, she'd had a vague idea that perhaps their castle had fallen, and everyone had moved on. She hadn't realised it had been so final and destructive.

Lissa pointed over to the left, toward some jagged peaks on the horizon. "The Kingdom of Stones. That's the only kingdom you can see from here. You'll meet the rulers, Sten and Ruby, soon."

For once, Lissa was speaking to her as though she was an equal, and Ember appreciated it, although she was fairly sure it was only because Lissa didn't want to antagonise the princes. But her appreciation was short-lived as Lissa continued, "Be careful of them. Sten likes to collect pretty things."

Ember refused to rise to Lissa's mocking tone. "I don't think Cole will let him." There was more than a hint of smug possessiveness in her tone, and as predicted, Lissa's hackles rose.

"You can't possibly think Cole is serious about you. Your life is just an insignificant blip compared to ours. You are to us what a mosquito is to you. You will age, wither, and die, and Cole and I will still be young. For you, it might as well be that we live forever."

"Well," said Ember, her voice trembling. "That might be true, but Cole wants me here. And I want to support him. And perhaps, when the tournament is done, he might ..."

Lissa let out a peal of laughter. "Keep you on? I doubt it. And if you were thinking of anything other than the sticky marshmallow between your legs, you'd leave him alone to focus on the tournament. Your world is tied to ours, and both our fates are in the games."

"How do you mean?"

"Haven't you noticed how your world is heating as it comes close to ours? The polar ice is melting, ocean temperatures are killing all the darling water creatures, uncontrollable fires are swallowing up swathes of forest; your world is nearing the point of no return. And it's all because the kingdom hasn't yet crowned the Sword. When Cole wins the tournament and becomes ruler, the veil between our worlds will grow thicker, temperatures will fall, and Earth may yet have a chance to redeem herself. But not if you continue getting in his way. He must win. For your sake as well as ours." It was clear Lissa was telling the truth. Sincerity oozed from every word she spoke. She came closer to Ember and finished with a short and vicious, "So stay away."

Ember looked out over Lissa's shoulder at the beautiful, alien vista in front of her, spread like a rumpled coverlet in shades of emerald green. The scented breeze swirled her skirts pleasantly around her ankles and her skin was deliciously moist and cool from the drifts of spray rising from the waterfall. She thought of Cole, and she knew she had never felt more beautiful, nor more desired in her life. What did the real world hold for her, anyway? Endless struggle for meagre wages to pay for poky housing, a run-down car, and chain store clothes made from sweatshop labour and pollutants. Even after art school, she wouldn't be able to live the life she deserved, not a life like this. And there was no one who was like Cole. No one.

She let her gaze rest on Lissa's beautiful face. She felt sorry for her, and she wanted the other woman to know how she felt. "I can't." There was a gentle sincerity in her voice. "I'm so sorry, but I can't."

Lissa's brows drew together in a savage scowl. Her nostrils flared, lips peeled back from her teeth and the gills in her neck opened wide to reveal the inner red of her throat. For an instant, she looked monstrous, terrifying. Without a word, she seized Ember's shoulders in a powerful grip and propelled her backward. For a moment, Ember teetered on the edge of the riverbank. Beyond, the water thundered and frothed. And then she fell.

CHAPTER 20

For a breathless few seconds, the current swept Ember away, and then the world disappeared as she plummeted into the heart of the falls. She just had time to suck in a horrified breath to scream, but then the water took her, and she spluttered and coughed, wondering if she was going to be the first person ever to drown in mid-air. The water slowed her descent, but tumbled her around and about, and for a moment she didn't know which way was up. And then, with a terrific splash, she plunged into the pools below.

The volumes of water shoved her under, holding her fast and she struggled and thrashed as the falls tumbled her relentlessly in a maelstrom of bubbles and froth. But her swimming training took over, and she reacted instinctively, diving even lower into the cloudy depths to escape the churning waters.

Her long skirts, so pretty and light above ground, were nothing but a hindrance in the water. They tangled about her legs, heavy and clinging, threatening to drag her down even further. But she was strong, she was used to the water, and she'd taken every swimming course that her job had offered, from lifesaving techniques to beginners' scuba. She wasn't panicked any more. Instead, her focus was solely on two things: one, getting herself into safety, and two, finding Lissa and punching her as hard as she could.

Before long, she was away from the thunderous tattoo of the falls above and into calmer waters, and she swam for the surface. The lungful of air she'd taken was a while ago now. Black spots were dancing before her eyes. She swam and kicked, and eventually broke the surface, gratefully sucking in a deep breath, and then another.

A tight grip on her ankle yanked her under the water again. She kicked out and struggled, but the grip was unyielding. When she saw the green creature with pointed teeth, scaly skin, and a long whipping tail, she almost screamed, but she kicked again, getting her foot in its face. It fell back, its grip loosened, and she broke free.

She swam for the surface again, grabbed another sputtering breath, and then she was under, flailing against the creature who had her by the skirt this time. She twisted a hand behind her back and fumbled at the ribbon holding the waist of her skirt. The fabric fell away as she kicked, tangling the creature in its folds and she had a sudden urge to wrap the skirt around its neck and choke the life out of it. Instead, she headed for the surface again. She'd just taken a breath when there was a splash next to her and she cried out and took a few hurried strokes before she realised Ashe was there.

His muscular arms came about her, and he attempted to bring her to shore, but she pushed him away, weary but still capable of getting herself to the bank.

"There was a ... a thing ..." she spluttered when she could speak. "Down there."

He dove again. A flash of blinding green lit up the pools, and then he was at her side. A few seconds later, a charred body rose to bob on the surface, the remains of Ember's shredded skirts still wrapped around it, melted into its scaly skin. The corpse drifted to the side of the pool, nudging at the rocks, and then to her horror, something dune-coloured and enormous with too many legs came bounding out of the trees, scooped it up and threw it into a cavernous maw, before disappearing again. The whole incident had taken only seconds, and she gasped and spluttered, swimming hard for the shore, wanting to put as much distance between her and the many-legged thing as possible.

When she got to the edge and dragged herself out onto the grass, she was shaking.

Ashe came beside her and waved a hand, casting some sort of invisible barrier between them and the mist that churned up from the falls. In an instant, she was dry but still cold and shivering from shock. He conjured a soft blanket of black fur and draped it around her, concealing her bare thighs. She nestled into its folds, unable to say anything, and he handed her a crystal glass containing some kind of warm, spicy drink. She drank deep, the tension loosening within her. When she felt she could speak without her voice breaking, she said, "Thank you."

"Perhaps next time you could swim in the castle lake. It's free of vermin."

Her shocked laugh held an edge of hysteria. "Believe me, I wasn't planning on going swimming. Lissa pushed me."

Ashe pressed his lips together as though to prevent a grin, and indignantly she dug him in the ribs. "Don't! I nearly drowned!"

"I apologise," he said, but his eyes danced. "Lissa has always had a fiery streak."

"She's a bitch," Ember said frankly, and this time Ashe laughed aloud. It was a pleasant laugh, she thought, spontaneous and free. He didn't look half so intimidating when amused.

"Cole won't be happy with her," was all he said, and then his face closed over again, and his eyes became shadowed.

She shivered and took another sip of the wine. "What was that thing that grabbed me? And what was that thing that grabbed it?"

"The leggy thing was a spider -"

"A spider! You must be joking."

"Why would I?"

"Spiders are ... little."

"*You* must be joking."

She let out a surprised laugh. "Your spiders are not like our spiders. Thank goodness."

"It must have come over the wall. The guards have not been vigilant. That will be remedied."

"And what about the water thing?"

"A type of scylla—a distant cousin of water sprites. There are a lot of them living in these pools. They're vicious. Not too bright. It was a clever idea, trapping them with your skirts."

His eyes drifted down to the length of her legs, and even though the blanket concealed every inch of skin, she couldn't help but blush. She wondered what he was doing there, and why he had even bothered to jump in and save her. He obviously didn't approve of her. Besides, if he had let her drown, it would have rattled Cole and wouldn't Ashe do everything he could to upset his rival before the tournament? It was beyond her reasoning. He had almost killed her on Earth, and now he was saving her life.

"I'll need a new skirt, if that's alright." He nodded, and she peeked under the blanket to see a new skirt, similar to the last, covering her lower half. "Thank you." She swallowed the last of her drink. "I suppose I'd better go back to the training ground. Cole will wonder where I am."

"No, he won't," said Ashe. "He's focused on Swirl."

His tone was lazy, and it irritated her. Why wouldn't Cole wonder where she was? And what would Lissa say to him?

"Nothing captures Cole's attention for long," he continued. "He gets, he discards. He's fickle."

"Cole cares about me," she said with conviction. "He told me."

"I have no doubt. When he's in the moment, he loves everything he's doing. But there's always another moment, always something else to do."

Offended at his intimation that she was that something, Ember pushed the blanket off her and got to her feet, hoping her knees wouldn't start shaking again. "Then I'm going back to the castle."

Ashe raised an eyebrow and got to his feet. "Not hastening to your lover's side?"

"You just said he was focused on training." She injected a careless tone into her voice, but it did sting to know that Cole was so preoccupied he might not even notice if she was there or not. "I'd just be in the way. Besides, I have no wish to see Lissa right now. I might push her off a cliff too."

Ashe smiled. "I believe you would."

He gave her a courteous bow before pressing the back of her hand to his lips. To her surprise, she felt a languid, mellow warmth spread through her, not a quickening of lust like that inspired by Cole's touch, but a steady glow that thawed her from the inside like a glass of sweet fae wine.

She snatched her hand away. "Don't do that."

He raised an eyebrow and shrugged. "I'll send a guide."

He vanished then, and the barrier was gone, the mist falling upon her and making her skirts damp. A yellow ball of light appeared, and she slowly followed it back up the path winding through the cliffs, and back to the castle.

CHAPTER 21

L ily's unspoken outrage lasted right through the time it took Ember to have a warm bath and get changed into a fresh outfit.

"I apologise," Ember said, when Lily had finally tweaked the last lock of hair into place. "I should have called you, like you said. I was just fed up, I guess."

"You also insulted one of the prince's mistresses and she threw you off a waterfall," Lily said. "And then you nearly died after being attacked by a scylla."

A thought struck Ember, and she said, "Does my behaviour reflect on you?"

To her chagrin, Lily, tight-lipped, nodded. "They'll say I'm not looking after you properly."

"And I'll say you are! Besides, I suppose I'm one of the prince's mistresses now too, so that must mean something."

She bent and called to her puppy, which she'd decided might as well be Rufus, and when he darted to her, wagging his little mop of a tail, she buried her face in his soft fur. "I really am sorry, Lily. I'll tell the prince it was my fault. If he asks," she added. After what Ashe had told her, she was unsure whether Cole would care.

She played with Rufus for a time, and after he fell asleep in his basket, leaned on her elbows at the windowsill, gazing over the twilight gardens. She would do some painting, she decided. Her nerves still jangled from the events of the day, and she longed to lose herself in the simple art of creation.

Lily accompanied her to the forest and when they got there, she asked a servant for her easel to be set up by Alena's pool of water, thinking that the surface ripples and reflections and silver light might prove to be a wonderful source of inspiration. On impulse, she asked for another easel for Lily. Lily protested, but Ember encouraged her to choose a brush and start painting.

"Just paint anything," she said. "You can splash it, smear it, make fingerprints, anything."

The brush dangled from Lily's fingers as she considered the canvas, and then she shook her head. "I cannot." She didn't sound sad or frustrated. She just said it. "It's not possible for me."

Ember frowned, unsure of what to say. "It might bore you, just standing around watching me paint." She didn't like to point out that she would feel uncomfortable having Lily stand over her shoulder while she worked, but Lily seemed to understand what she was getting at. After extracting a solemn promise that Ember would call if anything happened, she wandered off and Ember got to work.

The waterfall that slowly appeared on her canvas was what she remembered of the Falls, but without it in front of her, she couldn't hope to replicate it. She thought she might have the essence of it though, a tumbling column wreathed in rainbows and mist, crashing into a silver pool below. There was none of the fear as she had fallen along its length, just a sense of grandeur and wonder. Perhaps this was therapy, she mused. Feel the fear and paint it away.

She lost herself in her work, intent on making the water look as real as possible, when a violent stirring in the pool startled her. Up popped a green scaly head, which resolved itself into the figure of Alena. She stepped up onto the bank, shaking the last drops of water from her dress. Ember wondered if the cosy grandmotherly form was a glamour put on strictly for her benefit, and she was grateful. She couldn't chat idly with a lizard as tall as she was.

Alena studied the picture closely, eyes narrowed. "It reminds me of something, but I can't think what." She gestured, and the water jerked into motion, tumbling down the rocks. "That's better. It's the Falls, isn't it?" but at Ember's strained expression, returned the painting to its static self and added somewhat tartly, "If you don't like the glamour, then why do you wear one?"

Ember glanced down at her skirts, momentarily forgetting she had already changed out of the ones that Ashe had conjured for her. But had those not been real? Had she been walking around in just her underwear without knowing it? She'd passed a good few fae as she'd returned to the castle from the Falls, but they'd all avoided her as usual. None had smirked or whispered behind their hands, and besides, Lily would have said something.

"Not your dress, dear," Alena said. "That thing around your neck."

Ember's hand flew up to her gold and diamond necklace. She remembered how its appearance had wavered and changed in her bathroom mirror, but it remained reassuringly cold and unyielding under her fingers, like smooth metal, not leather. She tried to unfasten it at the back but couldn't manage it, and eventually Alena removed it from her neck with one careless crook of her finger.

It tumbled through the air and landed on the mossy grass, diamonds winking in the light. But then it flickered, transforming into a collar, like one a dog would wear, of black leather studded with flat beads of silver. She blinked, and it became a bejewelled chain of gold again, but the leather still showed underneath, as if the gold were merely painted over the top.

"Very good," said Alena, with approval. "Humans can't usually unsee a glamour."

"It was a present," Ember said, a bitter twist to her mouth. "I thought it was diamonds. I've never had a diamond anything before."

"Oh, don't worry about that," said Alena. "Diamonds are as plentiful as dust. Can't humans make them in laboratories? A diamond's only value is its marketing campaign."

Ember let out a surprised chuckle. What on earth would Alena know about laboratories and marketing campaigns? But her fleeting amusement didn't lessen her confusion. Cole had given her a collar as a gift. Why? Because he considered her a pet? A little dog to keep amused with toys and attention?

Alena watched the play of emotions across her face. "Cheer up. Look. I'll give you a much better present. What do you think of this?"

She made a pass in the air, and a paintbrush appeared in her hand. She handed it to Ember. It was surprisingly heavy, and the bristles were soft and full.

"Fallen baby centaur eyelashes," said Alena, watching Ember stroke the bristles. "Full of magic. Now you can make your own glamours."

Ember gasped, her eyes widening. "Seriously?"

"Try it!" Alena urged. "Run it along your waterfall."

Ember did so and gave a cry of delight as the water flowed down into the pools below. She swept the brush the other way and smiled, delighted, as the water changed direction and ran up the cliff face. "Can I glamour something else?"

She bent to the grass and carefully painted a stylised daisy, and there it was, in the peacock colours she had imagined, growing from the earth as though it had sprung from a tiny seed. She stepped back and admired her work. "Can you see that?"

"Yes," said Alena, unimpressed. "If you glamour it, you can decide who will see it as real."

"Thank you." Ember was deeply touched. "I think this is the nicest present I've ever had."

It was true. Ember hadn't had many presents in her life. She admired the brush a little longer and then placed it carefully in her pocket, not wanting to get it mixed up with her normal paint brushes.

"Alena," she said, changing the subject. "Someone told me that Earth is getting warmer because the kingdom hasn't yet chosen a Sword. Is that true?"

"All the kingdoms play a part in Earth's fortunes. If there is strife in the Kingdom of Skies, expect cyclones and storms on Earth. The Seeds spread pestilence and disease; the Sands pollute Earth's atmosphere. The Stones influence your politics and governance."

"And what about the Shields?" said Ember, thinking of the fallen column at the heart of the forest. She felt instinctively that its presence was vital to the fae, although she couldn't articulate why or how. Just as she had painted their column as complete, the kingdoms seemed incomplete without it.

"The Shields are aligned to human progress," Alena replied. "When the Shields fell, human enlightenment came to a halt."

Ember frowned. "What do you mean? We progress. Stuff gets invented all the time. Computers and apps and things."

"Progress of the human spirit. Prejudice, phobias, hatred. All grow unchecked without the Shields' protection."

"Oh. That's not good. For us ... and for you."

"The Swords instigated it. The Swords finished it. Step wisely, little one." Alena toed the necklace with a graceful foot shod in shimmering green. "You'd best put that on again, before they discover you've seen through their trick."

Wearing the necklace was the last thing Ember wanted to do, but she complied, fastening the catch with begrudging fingers. Although the necklace hadn't changed in size, it felt too snug. She swallowed, resenting its press against her throat.

"This place isn't safe for you," Alena warned, dissolving molecule by molecule. "But come and visit me again... if you don't die."

CHAPTER 22

As Ember followed Lily back to her room, she had the impression that the castle was busier. In the common areas, dozens of fae servants hurried about, ferrying bundles of linen and mysterious boxes to who knew where. In Cole's domain however, the halls were at peace, everlasting candles flickering gently, twilight pressing against the windows like a soft blanket. The gloom grated on Ember's nerves, oppressive and somehow menacing. What was wrong with sunlight? Perhaps too much sunshine would cause Cole to melt or catch fire and that's why he had made everything shadowed and dark.

"No, that's vampires," she said aloud, and Lily paused, throwing her a quizzical glance. "Never mind."

There came the sound of marching feet and she turned, thrown to see Lissa, flanked by several guards in full military uniform, marching toward her. Grudging relief passed over Lissa's face and she gestured at Ember, saying to the guards, "There. I knew we'd find her," and then to Ember, "Where have you been?"

"What do you care?" said Ember, hardly able to believe her ears. "You could have killed me!"

"I know. I'm rather surprised I didn't. Still, all's well that ends well. For you, that is." Her tone was flippant, but she wasn't quite her usual cocky self and there were livid bruises on her wrists, as though someone had grabbed and held her while she struggled. "You'll come with me now. The prince will be eager to see you. He's had all the guards out searching for you. Is it true when humans die, your body just ... rots? Revolting." She gave a delicate shudder and then jerked her head at Lily. "Get out."

Lily gave Ember a quick, apologetic glance and scuttled off, but in her anger, Ember barely noticed.

"Never mind me. You say you support Cole, yet you'd do that to him? Distract him, make him worry about me so soon before the tournament? That's a terrible thing to do."

Ashe might have told Cole she was unhurt, but naturally, he would have used her disappearance to upset his rival and gain advantage. Ember had played into his hands all too well. The idea upset her. She was Team Cole, not Team Ashe. She should have gone to Cole immediately to tell him she was okay. It was all her fault. The collar around her neck suddenly felt comforting and warm, and abstracted, she stroked it.

Lissa said nothing more, but turned on her heel and strode down the hall in the opposite direction, the guards falling back and waiting for Ember to catch up. The guide bobbed up and down uncertainly, and Ember called to it over her shoulder, "Sorry! See you later." Holding her skirts up out of the way, she rushed after Lissa, and the group hurried through the castle.

They came to the doors of the magnificent ballroom, where Ember had first met Cole. The waiting guards flung the doors open and Lissa swept through, Ember trailing in her wake.

Unlike before, the room was empty, save for a few servants and guards. Cole sat on the great white throne on the dais, chin in his hand, grimmer than Ember had ever seen him. When he saw her, his eyes lit up, and he leaped to his feet, moving to her.

"Your Highness!" Ember said, and that was as far as she got before he crushed her in his embrace. He kissed her forehead, her eyelids, and then her lips, and then pulled back, green eyes searching her face.

"But you look well! Not a scratch."

"I had a slight tussle with a ..." she couldn't remember the name for a moment, "a scylla, but I got away. I'm not a bad swimmer."

She was loath to mention that Ashe had blasted the poor creature into a charred corpse. She had a feeling Cole wouldn't like it. A glint showed in Lissa's eyes however, as though she had picked up on something in Ember's tone and suspected Ember was hiding something.

"Lissa should not have done that to you," Cole said, without so much as a glance at Lissa. "She will be punished. And then perhaps she will remember that she does not interfere in matters of the throne, no matter how important she thinks herself."

Lissa whipped her head up, hands upturned in appeal. "Your Highness, I apologise again. I can only say that I did what I did, to protect you and the Swords. This... creature... is disloyal and —"

"Disloyal?" shouted Cole, glaring at her, and instantly the servants and guards fell to one knee, heads bowed to the ground. The silence was absolute. A chill of fear crept over Ember, turning her stomach to knots. "When she wears my mark? How can she be? She is mine!"

There it was again, that presumption that she could be owned. And what mark was he talking about? But she wasn't about to interrupt Cole when he was like this. She felt an overpowering urge to sink to the floor as well, avert her eyes from him, make herself as small as she could so that his fury would pass over her. But to her grudging admiration, Lissa held herself motionless, as though Cole's temper were of no consequence at all. She hadn't even flinched.

"Come," said Cole to Ember and held out a hand. She took it with trembling fingers, and he led her up on to the dais. He arranged himself on the throne and pulled her onto his lap. She sat gingerly on his knee, looking down into the ballroom. Lissa stood alone on the floor below them.

"Lissa," Cole said in a grave tone. "You have caused grievous harm to the throne, and you shall suffer the consequences. Ten lashes."

For the first time, a look of fear passed over Lissa's face, and Ember felt a wave of pity for the girl. She whispered to Cole, "Your Highness, it's alright, I'm fine. Maybe just a telling off? She was just cross. Don't hurt her, please."

"Your mercy does you credit," Cole said, and his hand snaked around her waist, drawing her closer to him, so that her back rested against the broad warmth of his chest. His fingers angled themselves in her skirt and brushed against the warmth between her legs. She squirmed, wondering if anyone in the hall could see this, but all had their eyes to the ground, even Lissa, and no one was paying any attention. He pressed harder, his fingers stroking her, and her muscles clenched with pleasure beneath his hand. He lowered his voice and murmured in her ear, "A merciful princess. A merciful queen."

Two guards brought over a purple velvet-covered bench from the side of the room. One forced Lissa to her knees and pushed her down so that her torso rested on the bench, head hanging low. Then he took her dress at the neck and tore it off.

The delicate fabric came apart easily in his hands, baring the length of her back and the top of her buttocks. Her skin showed the tracing of light shadowed marks across it, the scales of her heritage. Lissa raised her head and gazed up at Cole. Her eyes were liquid with pleading, and even in her awkward position, she still gave an air of grace and beauty.

"Your Highness, any injuries to me could jeopardise my standing in the tournament," she began.

"It had better not," Cole snapped. He crooked a finger to another guard, who immediately came forward, although with his head averted, he couldn't possibly have seen Cole's gesture. The guard's gloved hand went behind his back, drawing forth a long leather whip tipped with gold tassels. He coiled the end around his fist and let the length hang, the braided leather swinging slowly, back and forth.

"You can't choose this... this *human*, over me," Lissa cried, her control slipping for the first time.

"It's none of your business whom I choose," said Cole, and as if to make his point, put a gentle hand to Ember's face and kissed her full on the mouth, a deep, passionate kiss that made her melt into him, arching her hips against his hand. When he pulled away, his eyes glittered, his mouth curved into a smile. He didn't take his eyes off Ember as he said slowly, "Perhaps, after the tournament, when I'm the Sword, I'll make her fae, and then she can stay forever."

Ember gazed back at him, her eyes wide. Become fae? All thoughts of home flew out of her head. All she saw was Cole, the dimples in his cheeks, his eyes burning into hers. She kissed him again, harder, her tongue deep in his mouth, as though they were the only two in the hall. He slipped a hand under her dress, and she parted her legs, wanting to give him easier access to her slick heat. She'd forgotten about Lissa, forgotten about everything but the wild desire building within her under his teasing fingers.

There was a whistle of air, a loud crack, and then Lissa cried out in pain.

Ember jerked away from Cole as though torn from a slumberous dream. A bloodied welt showed stark against Lissa's skin as the guard raised the whip again.

"No," Ember cried, and half rose from Cole's lap in protest, but Cole dragged her back again, his grip unrelenting.

He whispered in her ear, and despite the horror she felt at seeing Lissa beaten, the warmth of his breath sent pleasurable shivers down her back as he murmured. "No. You watch."

He licked her earlobe and kissed her neck, and her head fell back against his shoulder. She tried to close her eyes, tried to turn away from Lissa, writhing and crying out with every harsh crack of the lash, but she couldn't. She could hardly even think straight anymore. Cole's hands were all over her now. He pushed the lace of her underwear to one side and dipped his fingers into her wetness before sliding them up to caress the hot bud of her clitoris, gently at first and as she moaned, with a steady deliberate rhythm. Two fingers slid into her, just a little, making her buck her hips, wanting him deeper. The length of his cock was hard against her, and images flew through her fevered mind, of her settling before him and running her lips and tongue over him, here in front of everyone. Her hands slipped down to caress him, and he growled approvingly. He kissed her again, and again the whip came down.

He's getting off on this, she thought, with the dim rational part of her brain that was growing more muddled with every caress of Cole's hands, every kiss he took from her. And then, like a slap in the face, she realised, *and so am I.*

The thought of being aroused by this, by this *torture*, was horrifying, instantly sobering, and with a momentous effort, she pushed away from Cole, shaking her head. "I don't want this."

Cole's eyes glittered and he let her up, doing nothing to stop her as she stumbled down off the dais, and fled the hall, but she heard his words as if they were being whispered in her ear.

"Yes. You do."

CHAPTER 23

S he ran through the halls as if she were being chased, the sound of the whip and Lissa's cries echoing in her mind. The heat that had flooded her body when she was with Cole had vanished and, in its place, grew a gnawing, cold emptiness. She disgusted herself, revolted with the feelings he had engendered within her so easily, even as someone else was being hurt in front of her.

Her fingers shot up to the collar around her neck, and she plucked at it fruitlessly, eventually slowing to a walk so that she could release the catch. She held it in her hand for a moment. It was all leather now, with no hint of the gold and diamond necklace it had once been. She chucked it into a pot of roses standing in a little alcove. She wouldn't wear that thing ever again.

With its removal, her mind felt clearer, her purpose solidified. She had to get out of there. She didn't want Cole to make her fae. Perhaps if she just stayed out of sight, she'd be out of mind. The tournament was drawing close. That might be enough to keep him occupied.

She broke into a trot again, down one corridor and then another, not sure where she was or where she should go. Eventually, she stopped, heart pounding, and leaned against the wall. Who was she kidding? There was nowhere she could go where he wouldn't find her. This was his world, and he was all powerful in it. She had no allies and no way out. All she could do was play along, keep on his good side. Not that he'd ever tried to hurt her. He'd always been kind and considerate. But then, Lissa was his lover and teammate. She was worth more to him than Ember was, and yet he'd just had her whipped, as though she meant nothing. And if he could behave that way to Lissa, what did that mean for her?

She whispered for a guide and when the little light came, she followed it through the warren of halls back to her room. Little Rufus greeted her with endearing yelps and much wagging, and she hugged him close, hoping the warmth of his body might chase away the chill that seemed to have settled into her bones. Seeing how upset she was, Lily begged to help, and as an act of rebellion, Ember asked her for a pair of jeans and tee shirt to wear, instead of "all this frilly stuff." Lily frowned at that but went into the bathroom to turn on the taps, while Ember stripped, keen to do nothing more than wash the disturbing day off her and climb between crisp cool sheets.

The water was refreshing, and she washed her hair and brushed her teeth before dousing herself with her favourite scent. Lily had left a robe for her, and she tied it around her, wrapped a towel around her head, and walked into her room, halting abruptly when she saw Cole standing by the window. Lily and the puppy were nowhere in sight. A new wooden chest studded with silver stood in the corner, carved with elegant images of people and fae intertwined in an eternal embrace.

"Do you like your room?" he said conversationally, looking out at the view. "I thought you might like a view of the gardens."

"It's lovely," she said. She didn't know what to do, but thought she might try to act naturally, and so she tugged the towel from her head and moved to the dressing table for her brush. She dragged it through her hair mechanically, unable to look at him. He had appeared casual enough, but underneath, Ember sensed an energy that he was keeping in check, something dangerous.

"It's too light," he said, and the room darkened, candles springing into flame. The scent of spicy musk seeped into the room, cloying and seductive. His voice took on a lilting tone. "The banishment of light brings forth greater mysteries, don't you think? Secrets and shadows, a cloak of enchantment ..."

"How is Lissa?" she asked when his voice trailed off. She was trying for lightness, but her voice wobbled, and she bit her lip.

"She's learned her lesson."

He crossed the room in a few strides, and she backed up. He stopped short, as if aware he had scared her, and looked at her intently, his expression serious. "She could have killed you. I would have thought you'd be happy that I punished her."

"You didn't have to hurt her."

"No," he agreed, and there came something feral in his eyes. "But sometimes, we can only learn lessons through physical chastisement. My people will do what they want, and so I will do as I must." He held up his hands, palms facing in an act of supplication. "But for your sake, my darling, I shall not do it again."

She glanced up at him, her heart breaking a little with the words, 'my darling'.

"Do you mean it?"

He shrugged. "I said so, didn't I?"

He held out his hands to her, and she moved forward to him. She didn't show any hesitancy. She was aware she had to play along for the sake of her own survival. He could banish her to a dungeon if he wanted to, he could have her beaten, he could reduce her to a lump of charred smoking meat. She was afraid, but she was even more afraid to show him her fear. And so, she smiled and took his hands and allowed him to draw her into his arms.

He brushed his lips across her forehead, and then held out something to her, a gold and diamond necklace with a shadow of black leather beneath. "You took it off."

"I ..." she didn't know what to say. The sight of it made her feel cold all over again. If she said it fell off, would he know she was lying? "It felt too tight. And I was cross."

He stroked a link, and it divided into two, making the necklace a little longer. "Will you wear it for me now?"

What could she say? "Of course."

He kissed her on the lips, and a warm glow rapidly replaced the chill. His tongue slipped inside her mouth, and he kissed her properly, his hands sliding down her back to grasp her buttocks, pulling her closer. The intoxicating scent of spice intensified, making her head swim. She melted against him, kissing him back with increasing abandon. He broke the kiss, and while she struggled to regain her senses, put the necklace around her throat and fastened it. It felt right. She touched it, liking the way it settled across her collarbone, cooling against her heated skin.

"Now, Ember," he said, and tugged at the tie fastening her robe, drawing one shoulder of her robe to the side, and then the other. It slipped off and puddled on the floor, leaving her standing naked in front of him. "We have to talk about something."

"What?" she said. She didn't want to talk. She wanted him to touch her. All she could think about was his hands, his mouth, and his...

He crossed over to the chest and flicked open the catch. The lid flew open. She craned to see, but it was too dark to discern anything inside. He reached in and brought out two long ribbons, glistening smooth as silk in the dim light.

"Lessons must be learned."

Her mouth sagged, and she took a step back. "What's that?"

He moved to her, looping a ribbon around first one wrist, and then the other. She tried to pull away, but he crooked a finger, and the ribbons came to life, tugging her to the bed, as if she were a dog on a leash.

"Lie down."

She demurred, shaking her head, and he slid a hand behind her head, into her mass of wet hair and pulled it. Hard. "Lie down."

Without a word, she sat on the edge of the bed, drawing her legs up beside her. Her scalp was tingling with pain, but already her nipples were hard and aching, a familiar molten excitement building deep inside. The arousal he had forced from her earlier washed over her again, and she was both eager and apprehensive. There was no tenderness in his mood. His expression was like granite, his thick cock firmly outlined against the silk of his pants.

He dragged her up the bed, forcing her onto her belly, and the ribbons tied themselves to the posts of the bed. She tugged against them, but the ribbons resisted, the knots drawing ever tighter. He strolled to the chest, retrieving two more.

"Spread your legs."

She did so, wondering if he could see the glistening wanting between her folds. The ribbons rippled through the air, swooping down to lash her ankles to the bottom posts of the bed.

His gaze made her feel exposed, embarrassed. "Cole," she began, and then his broad hand connected with her bottom.

The sting from the sharp smack came a second after the crack of sound reverberated throughout the room, and she sucked in an outraged breath, and reared up, pulling against the silk ribbons.

"Be quiet. Lie still."

He struck her again and again. She wriggled and squirmed, trying to escape his hand, but it was impossible. Her buttocks felt as though they were on fire. His hand came down again, a stinging slap, even more forceful than the rest, and she cried out.

"I told you to be quiet."

She felt him move away, and turning her head, watched him walk to the chest and dip inside. Another ribbon, this one thick and short, came to her, whipping itself around her face, covering her mouth and tying at the back of her head, smothering all sound.

When he drew out a short-handled whip with tasselled ends, a wave of fear came over her and she yanked at the ribbons, desperate to free herself.

"Your skin glows red, like a cherry," he observed, tapping the whip against his thigh. He sank onto the bed, and she flinched, but he merely smoothed his hand against her bruised flesh, leaning down to kiss first one cheek and the other. "It feels hot." He moved further down and then his hands were spreading her swollen labia, his tongue darting inside.

The pain immediately turned to pleasure, and she moaned, trying to spread her legs wider, her hips rising from the bed. He licked and suckled on her clit and then he spread her buttocks and lapped at her puckered hole, eliciting gasps and moans.

It was while she was still in a fever of arousal that he wielded the whip. If his hand had been hurtful, it was nothing compared to the sting of leather. She squealed as he whipped methodically and slowly, covering her arse and upper thighs with stroke after stroke, never in the same place twice, always keeping her guessing. And just when she thought she would scream with the agony of it, he would lick her and suckle her until she writhed in ecstasy. Her desire rose higher and higher, and just as she was at the peak, as she threatened to tip over the edge, he whipped her again.

It wasn't long before the cut of the leather tassels began to evoke new sensations, a twisted gratification, a maelstrom of dark sensuality. Mist coalesced around them, Cole's arousal a tangible force, as his arm came down, again and again, before his mouth was on her, teasing, tasting, followed by the cut of the lash. He was panting with it, his clothes gone, the length of his cock glistening at the head. Finally, he threw the whip aside and settled on his knees between her legs. She was sobbing, face damp with tears, throbbing with pain and incomplete desire. The ribbons loosened enough for him to pull her hips up, and a pillow slid underneath, giving her support.

When he finally slammed into her, she arched her back, submitting to every thrust, crying out his name. He fisted one hand in her hair, pulling her head back until she thought her spine might crack, and the other slipped around to squeeze her breast, cruelly pinching her nipple. She came and again, sparks exploding behind closed lids, and when he joined her, she collapsed.

The ribbons slid away, leaving her free, but helpless, overcome with gratified languor.

His voice was gentle, the words sounding as if they were coming from very far away.

"Who do you belong to?"

"You." Her answer was a breath, a sigh.

"Where do you live?"

"Here."

"Where did you come from?"

Th answer was hesitant. "I ... don't remember."

"Good."

She lay, her eyes closed, utterly drained. She didn't even have the energy to raise her head. The collar lay against her skin, warm and comforting, and she slept.

CHAPTER 24

S he woke to a soft twilight that was lighter than the whirling darkness of the night before. She stretched, her body aching and bruised, with stinging welts across her flesh from the whip that Cole had so expertly wielded.

Lily applied a soothing salve to her wounds, most of which Ember couldn't reach herself. The ointment vanished the welts immediately, but she could still feel the ache beneath her skin. She didn't care though; she fell on her breakfast with a hearty appetite, and when Lily showed her the pair of jeans and white tee she'd requested just hours earlier, she told Lily she'd changed her mind, that Cole preferred she wear pretty things. Without a word, Lily brought her a pair of flowing pants and silk shirt with a loose, cowl style neckline that offered glimpses of the shadowed cleavage between her breasts. Ember looked at herself in the bathroom mirror and smiled, admiring the way the deep blue of the fabric gave her skin a luxuriant glow and the way her diamond necklace glittered in the light. She felt pretty. She felt desired. She felt wonderful.

When she returned to the room, Lily was remaking her bed with fresh sheets, the old, rumpled ones dotted with blood, lying in a heap in the corner. Ember watched her fondly. She wanted to please her, to make her as happy as she was.

She went to the dressing table and drew out the brush that Alena had given her. "Lily. Come here, please."

Obediently, Lily left the bed and went to her side, a questioning look in her eyes. Ember bade her turn around, and untied the ribbons in the back of her tunic, revealing the remains of her poor ruined wings, the stumps scarred and knotted in vicious tones of pink and red. Carefully, Ember took her brush and painted an arching line from the tip of one broken wing, to a point high above Lily's head. She painted the wings in the manner of the other fae she had seen, gracefully arching up and then down again, almost to the floor. As she painted each feather, she imagined them in colours that would suit dark-haired Lily: royal blue, crimson, and emerald green tipped with glinting gold, the vivid, vibrant colours of a tropical bird. When she had finished, she gently turned Lily to face her. Lily's eyes were closed, a trickle of a tear oozing down her face.

"Oh no, what's wrong? Do you not like them?" said Ember in distress. She'd thought to please Lily, not cause her sorrow.

In response, Lily flexed her new wings, folding them around her like a cape, and then snapping them out wide with a clap of percussion. She leapt into the air and took a turn around the room, and then again, faster and faster, the candlelight in the room blown out in an instant, drapes flapping wildly, tiny fairy lights dancing like erratic dust motes through the room.

Ember laughed, clapping her hands, and Lily dived, stumbling as her feet touched the floor.

"I'm out of practice." She laid her palm against Ember's cheek and gave a watery smile. "Thank you. You don't know what this means to me."

Ember hastened to explain. "They're not real. They're just a glamour."

"They're real to me," and Lily took to the air again.

"You could take a turn around the gardens," Ember called to her. "If you're up high enough, no one will know."

Lily dropped by her side, a little out of breath, her landing a little surer. "Do you think so? If I get caught, I'll be in terrible trouble."

"Then I'll deal with them," said Ember, confidently. She had the ear of the prince, didn't she? She was going to be a fae herself. She was a royal mistress, a person of standing. All who feared Cole should fear her too, and the knowledge of it felt dark and pleasurable within her. "When you return, you can take the wings off and hide them away somewhere where no one will find them, if you like. Go, Lily. I'm going to go to the training grounds. You enjoy yourself and I'll see you later."

Lily threw her arms around Ember and kissed her on the cheek. "I will never forget this," she said seriously. "Never."

She skipped to the windows, hoisted herself up onto the sill, and leapt into the air. Ember rushed to the window and watched Lily dive low and then flick her wings out, gliding up over the gardens and then the trees, along the walled boundary of the castle and out of sight.

Seeing Lily so free and unencumbered gave Ember a delightful glow. She finished making the bed herself, and as she smoothed her hand over the silken sheets, she thought about what she had done in this bed, wondered if Cole too was remembering all that they had done the night before. The carved chest had vanished from the corner, and she wondered if she would see it again, *when* she would see it again. Life was long with the fae. She had found her prince, and she was going to live happily ever after.

The guide came as soon as she called, requesting it take her to Cole. It bobbed in acknowledgement and led her out of the castle and down a sunlit path through a vast apple tree orchard. Boughs bent with red fruit, each smooth-skinned and shiny, without flaw. She had assumed that Cole would be at the training grounds she had visited before, where the centaurs had thundered up and down the obstacle course, but this path led to a different place.

A tented marquee with a fringed silken roof sat on a soft green lawn. Inside the tent, soft cushions lay scattered around knee-high tables spread with silver dishes of fruits and sweets, and bottles of wine with drops of condensation beading the glass. Lots of fae were there, reclining, laughing, and chatting, wings folded and tucked, jewels glittering in the sunshine.

Beyond the marquee stood two hills on either side of a gully, and in the skies between, were what looked like a flock of birds, whirling and diving. Ember halted, not sure what to do. She couldn't see Cole anywhere, and she hadn't yet met any other fae apart from Lily. She hadn't tried either because they all turned away from her when she approached. Even so, her humanity was a novelty, and perhaps they wouldn't be unkind to her if they knew their Prince had an interest in her. Thankfully, as she drew closer, she recognised Swirl, standing with a group of centaurs at the side of the marquee.

He turned as she approached and smiled in greeting. "Have you come to watch the Eagles fly?" His voice was sonorous, drawing the attention of the nearby fae. As they caught sight of Ember, they put their heads together, deep in gossip. Some flicked her hostile glances, and she guessed they knew what had happened to Lissa.

"I came to find Cole," she said, relieved that there was at least one friendly face there.

"He flies too," said Swirl. "There, look?"

He pointed up to the clouds. Ember focused and then stared in open-mouthed awe. Winged fae rode winged horses through the sky, performing complicated manoeuvres, as if they were dancing. The skill the riders employed to prevent their wings colliding with those of their mount was enviable. Wings beat in tandem, keeping the riders balanced, even on the tightest of turns and the deepest dives. Cole was amidst them, easily recognisable as the only fae without wings of his own, and he rode a horse of pale gold with a white mane and tail, its majestic wings dark bronze.

"Don't be too impressed now," said Swirl, teasing. "A horse with wings is practically an insect."

The others with him laughed and nudged one another, but Swirl's flippant mockery was wasted on Ember. She watched with deep admiration as Cole's mount climbed higher and higher before making a steep dive through the gully. She thought it must be like heaven up there, bound by nothing but the open sky, and her fingers unconsciously went to her necklace, fiddling restlessly with the links.

"Would you like some wine?" said Swirl and snapped his fingers for a servant who was there in an instant, pouring Ember a crystal glass.

The bubbles danced merrily, the sweet fae wine warming her through as she sipped.

Over the rim of her glass, she saw Lissa standing alone on the other side of the pavilion. Ember had never seen Lissa alone before; it was as if the other fae were avoiding her. She didn't have the same aura of confidence that she'd had the first night Ember had met her, when the fae had fallen back from her left and right as though she were a grand ship parting the waves. She looked as though this was the last place she wanted to be, and it was only stubborn bravado keeping her there.

Ember hesitated a moment and then, murmuring a farewell to Swirl, approached her. Lissa watched her, nostrils flaring, dislike written all over her face, but she forced a smile and inclined her head.

"Good morning,"

"Good morning," Ember replied, and then in a rush, "I'm so sorry about what happened. I —"

Lissa raised a haughty eyebrow. "It's not your place to apologise for the prince's judgement. His word is law."

"I didn't mean that, exactly. I'm just sorry you got hurt."

"Don't worry about me." Her voice was brittle. "I'm tougher than I look."

She was using the exact words that Ember had once used to her, and Ember wasn't sure how to take that. Lissa gave an airy toss of her head, her tone becoming light.

"When I have helped him win the tournament, he will reward me. He won't forget me. Everything I have endured, that I have suffered, will have been worth it. His thanks will be immeasurable." She glared at Ember. "And if you do anything to impede that ..." she broke off, shaking her head with a wry chuckle. "Goodness. How quickly you arouse disdain. I wonder if that's a human trait? I'm trying to control it, but it's desperately difficult."

"Thanks," said Ember, tartly. Despite the pity she felt for Lissa, she felt an inordinate amount of dislike too. "Perhaps we should just stay out of each other's way?"

"Done!" said Lissa, and strode away, leaving Ember alone and feeling a little silly. She sipped her wine, but the sharp sweet tang had become acidic and unpleasant, and so she tipped it out, handing the glass to a passing servant.

She decided she'd go back to the castle, perhaps paint a little. If Alena was there, she could ask her what it meant to become fae. Would it hurt? Would she have to die to be brought back as a fae? No, that's vampires, she reminded herself.

There came a rushing of air behind her, followed by the thudding of a great weight. Cole slid from his mount, tossed the reins to a waiting servant and strode toward Ember, lifting her in his arms and kissing her.

She clung to him, her limbs becoming liquid, and he smiled beneath her lips, easing her away.

"Not now, my darling," he chided, and she smiled, delighted to be in his sight again. "You look very content. Not too sore?"

Heat rose to her cheeks, and she caught a sly smirk between a couple of fae who were blatantly eavesdropping nearby, but she shook her head. "No."

"Good. Would you like to ride?" He led her toward his horse, and she followed hesitantly, unsure of what he meant. "This is Farla." He took Ember's hand and let the mare take her scent, her soft lips nuzzling at Ember's palm. "There. Do you like horses?"

Farla eyed Ember as if she understood every word, and Ember hastened to reassure them both that yes, she loved horses, although she hadn't ridden one since she was a child.

After her parents died, the authorities had sent her to live with an elderly aunt who owned a small farm, with a few cows, a couple of friendly dogs, hundreds of chickens, and an equally elderly horse called Bob. Bob had been stoic and uncomplaining with the lonely girl, letting her climb aboard and ambling around the pasture under her direction, enjoying the apples and carrots she pilfered from the kitchen as payment for the patience he showed her. Her aunt was too old to manage the farm and her as well, and she'd only been there a few months before the authorities had come knocking again, the animals sold, the farm gone, the aunt placed in an old folk's home, and Ember sent to live in one of the first of many foster homes.

She hadn't thought about Bob in years, and the memory wasn't solid and concrete, just a vague jumble of images of warm summer sun, and the feel of Bob's broad back, the gentle brush of horse lips as he snaffled an apple, and then ... they were gone, as though it were a dream she'd had once a long time ago.

"I'm not sure if it's such a good idea." Falling from a normal horse was painful enough. If she fell from Farla's back, she'd likely die.

"There's nothing like it," Cole promised her, as a servant quickly strapped a new type of harness to Farla's saddle. "And I know you like being tied up," he added wickedly.

Ember gasped in delighted shock and tapped his wrist reprovingly. "Stop!"

He threw back his head and laughed and she laughed with him, noting that the surrounding fae were now all observing her high in

Cole's favour. Politically, it would be unwise to be rude to the prince's mistress even if she were a human, and more than one caught her eye and gave her a quick, ingratiating smile. Her spirits rose, and then sank again as Farla gave a loud whinny, shaking her mane as if impatient to be off. But Cole was in a good mood and the last thing Ember wanted was to spoil it, even if she was terrified. He helped her into the saddle and the servant buckled a belt across her lap, effectively binding her in.

"Be gentle, Farla," said Cole and gave her a slap across her rump.

The horse broke into a trot, the great wings flexed as she leaped, and Ember screamed as the ground fell away beneath her.

CHAPTER 25

At first, she was too nervous to look anywhere but Farla's mane blowing back in the breeze. She kept the reins loose and gripped tight to the pommel, trusting that the belt around her waist would keep her from falling. Farla flew so gently and sweetly along the gully, with none of the daring dives and swoops that the other horses were doing, that Ember's confidence soon rose, and she loosened her grip, sitting up straight and gazing around her.

A horse approached, pulling up alongside, sending Farla into a sidestep and making Ember clutch at the pommel again.

"Welcome to my home!" Broude shouted, waving an expansive hand. "Do you love it?"

"It's wonderful," she called back, and he wheeled and dived.

The tent seemed a long way away, and there was another at the far end of the gully that she hadn't noticed while on the ground. Unlike Cole's pavilion in cream and pale yellows, like shifting sand dunes in the desert, this one was squat and solid, in charcoal grey and midnight blue. Ember guessed immediately who it belonged to, and her lips pressed together in annoyance. Yes, if she had returned directly to Cole after the waterfall affair, he might not have been so upset, and he might not have hurt Lissa. But, if Ashe had told Cole where she was, that she was safe, perhaps none of it would have happened either.

Ember wasn't sure how to direct the horse; it somehow seemed impertinent to tug on Farla's reins or kick her in the sides, but Farla seemed to guess at the direction of her thoughts and cantered in a gentle curve away from the dark pavilion—only to be brought up short as another horse shouldered in front of her.

Farla came to an abrupt halt, and the belt tightened around Ember's waist as she jerked against it. She clutched at the pommel, but Farla's wings kept her steady, and she glared at the figure in black before her. "Watch it!"

Ashe gave her a mock salute, turning his horse next to hers, as companionably as if they were two friends out on a day's ride together. He rode as if his horse was an extension of himself, the black shimmer of its hide and wings, and silver bridle a match to Ashe's habitual uniform of black leather and burnished silver hardware.

"Don't be like that. You're the one who was coming to visit me."

"I was not! I was heading back, if you must know."

"Why?"

"Because you got me and Lissa into terrible trouble. Why didn't you tell Cole that I was safe?"

He shrugged. "Why should I?"

She let out an aggravated sigh. "He was furious."

"I heard." He smiled, as if the thought bothered him not a jot. "Fancy having his own teammate beaten."

His tone was careless, and in that instant, she hated him. The memory of the welts rising on Lissa's pale skin, and worse, the memory of the arousal Cole had kindled in her while it was happening, sickened her. And the way he said it, *teammate,* as if that were the problem, as if it would have been okay for the beating to be delivered to a servant. She couldn't think of anything to say, and his gaze flicked to her face, his expression taken aback, as though he had expected a careless answer in return.

"I forget you're not one of us. You must find us terribly... savage." His tone was cutting, and it was clear he didn't expect a response. "Don't fret. You'll be home before you know it. The opening ceremony begins soon, and then —"

"Home?" The word had evoked a strange feeling within her, a memory of a dream, like a horse she'd once had—or, no. It was gone. She frowned, puzzled.

Ashe's face darkened. "Ember? You've been with Cole again?"

She seized on that, the image of her time with Cole as sharp and clear as a shard of glass. "Oh, yes."

She smiled a slow, seductive smile of reminiscence that included Ashe, but had nothing to do with him at all, and he drew in a sharp breath. "Ember, you mustn't. He can be addictive, all the fae can, but he will take from you, and take, and take, and you'll be left with nothing. He'll suck you dry and leave a husk. It's what he does."

She looked at him with scorn. "You're just saying that to upset me, and to upset Cole. Your tactics won't work on me."

"Don't you want to go back to Earth? If you keep this up, you'll lose yourself, you know. You won't be anything."

"I'll be fae. And I can look at Earth in Cole's mirror any time I want."

She couldn't even think why she would want to. Why see a place that didn't have Cole in it?

"Cole's mirror ..." he said thoughtfully, and then with a braying snort, "Of course. That's how he found you. But why you?"

What he said barely registered. She had no idea what he meant, and after a moment, he gave a muttered command, sending his horse into an abrupt about-face, and flew off without another word. She didn't watch him go, just urged Farla to fly, faster and faster, back toward the distant tent, back towards Cole.

Farla landed gently on the green turf and gave a snort as if to say, "There you go."

Ember laughed and patted her neck, thanking her, as two servants rushed toward them, one taking Farla's bridle, the other unfastening Ember from her harness and helping her to the ground. Cole strode toward her, and she smiled, saying, "That was —"

She meant to say "fun" but one look at the dark expression on Cole's face and the words died on her lips. "What's happened? What's the matter?"

"I saw you talking with him. We all did."

She cast a quick glance around. All the fae nearby were silent, disapproving.

"I ..." she didn't know what to say. "He talked to me," she finished inadequately. "And I told him he should have told you I was safe that day at the waterfall."

As soon as she'd said it, she wished she hadn't. Cole's face closed over and he folded his arms, waiting for her to continue.

"He helped me with the scylla. He burned it."

She looked at the ground, unable to look him in the eye. It was a few moments before he spoke, and when he did, his voice was deathly quiet.

"Go back to the castle and wait for me there."

She didn't apologise. She said nothing at all. Instead, she did as he commanded and walked back to the castle alone, without even a guide to light the way.

Chapter 26

C ole kept her close after the training of the Winged Eagles, hardly able to bear having her out of his sight. When he was called
away on business, he set two guards and Lily to accompany Ember
wherever she went. He told her it was because a human might prove
too much temptation for a mischievous fae who wanted to cause strife,
but she suspected he just wanted to keep eyes on her. The constant
vigilance chafed on her and she longed to slip away unseen for a few
hours, but it was impossible. Training and entertaining filled the days,
and every night, there was a dinner or a dance. Afterwards, Cole took
her to his room. Some nights she didn't even feel as though she wanted
to have sex, but always, always, he would coax her into exploring new
heights of sensation and arousal. Some nights she cried with pleasure,
other nights she wept with pain, and in the morning, she was never
entirely sure which was which. He drank from her as though she were
the finest of wine and used her lust to satisfy his own. He couldn't get
enough of her. And with every night that passed, she lost a little more
to him, just as Ashe had warned.

The castle grew busier as guests arrived for the tournament. Fae thronged the halls and gardens, and servants rushed here and there. She learned to recognise the various kingdoms from the attire they wore. The Sands were always inadequately dressed in the briefest of gauzy clothing, with daggers at their hips and gold jewellery glinting on their fingers, ankles, wrists, and throats. Tall and lithe, dark-skinned with flashing black eyes, they were elaborately polite and spoke with a lyrical turn of phrase that always had two or three obscure meanings tucked into the folds of their expansive poetry.

The Skies were aloof and taciturn, bundled up in tunics and pants of fleece and down, bows and arrows tucked into quivers slung over their shoulders. They hastened in packs, ever watchful for danger, although Cole had assured her that there would be no bloodshed in the castle under orders of the Adjudicator. All who caused trouble would suffer his wrath. It did not surprise Ember that the Adjudicator's wrath didn't extend to her; Cole had told her bluntly that she roamed the halls at her own risk, hence the guards.

The Seeds were closest to her original idea of fairies. They lived deep in the jungles and Lily explained, with an air of superior disdain, that they didn't build palaces or even houses. They preferred to live in the open, moving along walkways strung between towering trees high in the forest canopy, and sleeping in mossy hollows and in hammocks under the stars. All wore soft fringed leather with silver tipped spears worn across their backs, and all were playful and light, prone to out-bursts of laugher and chatter. The women wore their hair shining and loose; the men were bare-chested and tattooed, and they were unin-hibited in all things: emotions, sex, conversation, feasting, dancing, killing. Even for fae, they seemed to wring every inch of pleasure from life, as though they measured their lives in units of enjoyment and the winner was the one who had the most fun.

She had met one ruler of the Stones, Sten, and had disliked him at first because he had immediately asked Cole if he could buy her. Cole had laughed at her outraged expression and told Sten that he couldn't afford Ember at any price. That didn't make her feel much better, but she had put on a pleasant smile so as not to offend this important guest, and when Cole was called away on some errand, she politely asked Sten if he wanted to see the gardens.

"Oh no," said Sten. "There's only one thing I want to see. The tree."

She took him to the hall where the flaming tree stood and as they walked, he made her laugh with some harmless gossip about the Skies. She found herself warming to him. He was a kind man, solidly built, with a grey beard and a silver crown set with rubies to honour his partner Ruby, the other ruler of the Stones. His grizzled locks were at odds with his skin, which was as smooth and unlined as any of the fae, and she felt he was very old, much older than Cole.

She hadn't been back to see the tree since that first time, but it was exactly the same, with branches and leaves that crackled and hissed. The heat from it fell across her like a warm caress and she moved closer to the tree, wanting to see the pendant up close. Sten hovered by the door, squinting against the heat.

"Come back," he called to her. "You're too pretty to scorch."

She turned, surprised to see him a few metres behind her with his entourage, and she retreated to his side, although the heat didn't bother her much at all.

"The winner of the tournament will be able to brave the fae fire and retrieve the pendant. Tana, the last Blade, is trapped in there still. He won't die until the new second replaces him."

Ember squinted at the pendant. She hadn't realised the Blade was still alive inside. Were the shifting shapes mere shadows cast by a fae trying to get free?

She shivered, despite the heat of the room, and Sten laughed. "I think the inside is quite comfortable. I'm told it's a palace, a luxurious place, albeit very quiet."

Sten decided he'd like to see the gardens after all, and they and their entourages wandered through the park-like setting, talking. Apparently, the gardens in the Kingdom of Stones were a rather rockier affair, only worth seeing at night.

"Isn't it dangerous, stumbling around on rocks in the dark?" she asked.

"Yes, but dragons roam the gardens during the day. Far more dangerous."

"Dragons?"

Sten burst out laughing at the incredulity on her face. "The ones in the grounds are small, but they can still set you aflame if you're not careful."

"Goodness!" Ember broke into startled laughter and Sten joined her, although his amusement appeared to be directed at her astonishment, rather than his words. That was where Cole found them, laughing together in a secluded part of the gardens, and his brows knit together in an increasingly familiar frown.

"You've been a time." He gave Sten a courteous bow, although it was shallow and perfunctory.

"We've been having a *delicious* time." Sten slipped his arm around Ember's waist and hugged her close. She watched uneasily as Cole fixed Sten with an icy glare, and gracefully slid from Sten's grasp with an apologetic smile, moving to Cole's side.

"Are you sure you don't want to give her up?" Sten said. "She's quite enchanting. I have a cave of gold with your name on it."

In response, Cole kissed Ember, hard and insistent, bending her back against his powerful arm as though she were pliant bamboo. She couldn't have escaped if she'd tried; his grip was unrelenting. She kissed him back, but there was something in it that felt repellent, forced, muting her usual automatic physical response. There was no melting of her loins, no rapid tattoo of her heart. Instead, she felt ... nothing.

Sten laughed, and Cole pulled away from Ember, his eyes glittering. "Tea is being served in the west wing dining room."

"I love tea," said Sten. "Are you joining us?"

"Oh no," said Cole, tucking Ember's arm under his and walking her off. "We have other things to do."

Ember twisted around to bid Sten farewell, but Cole jerked her back, and she returned her gaze to the path ahead. There was a familiar churning in her stomach, a sensation she hadn't felt since her time with ... with Bruno.

Cole was hurrying her, but she still heard Sten's deep chuckle and his remark, "You'd better hope he wins, Ember. Ashe won't want Cole's cast-offs."

CHAPTER 27

C ole used her in that moment, and afterwards, as she lay in the rumpled sheets, she wondered how long it had been since he had made her feel truly content. As always, her body was satiated, but her mind was restless, a flurry of thoughts and impressions, too ephemeral to pin down. The only images she could see clearly were that of the tree, the pendant, and Tana the Blade trapped inside.

She sat up and winced. The bites on her shoulder stung, and at once a maid was by her side, dabbing an ointment on that took away the fire but left an ache inside. A servant attended to Cole as well, and as he took a glass of wine, his face was grim.

"The Stones are against me," he said, as though they were already halfway through a conversation. "Sten has made that perfectly clear. And with the Stones go the Skies." He looked at her over the rim of his glass, at the maid brushing her hair so that it shone ebony black in the candlelight. "Are you not concerned?"

"Anything that concerns you, concerns me."

Her tone was reassuring, and he gave her an abstracted smile. It was true she was worried, but not about the same thing that worried Cole.

If what Alena had said was true, that the kingdoms had an influence on Earth, then a fight between the Skies, Stones and Swords could only spell disaster for her world, the world that was growing more distant and dimmer with every passing day. Every time Cole took her, she lost something. She was aware of it, a gnawing absence, but she couldn't recall that which she had already forgotten.

The maid brought her a robe, and she slipped it on as she rose from the bed to use the bathroom Cole had conjured especially for her. When she returned, she paused by the mirror and stroked a finger along the carved frame. It showed a cityscape, somewhere alive and vibrant, with tall buildings plastered with signs in a language she couldn't understand.

"Hong Kong," Cole said. "When I'm the Sword, we'll go there. We'll go everywhere. Nowhere will be forbidden to us, there will be no limits."

"Will you show me ..." she wanted to say home, but here was her home, wasn't it? "Show me where you found me?"

The mirror clouded and then came a picture, foggy and indistinct at first and then crystal clear. It was an unremarkable street, old houses with weather-beaten facades, dry weeds poking through cracks in the pavement. It looked untidy and unloved, as though those living there had given up a long time ago.

"I don't remember it." She tried to still the rising surge of panic within her. She should know this place, but she didn't.

"You don't remember it like this. It's been years there since I found you."

"Years?"

"Years and years."

"Oh."

So, time had moved on. She moved away from the mirror and sank onto the bed. She'd thought that by looking in, she would find something within herself, and yet she still felt empty and lost.

"Are you sad, my darling?" he said tenderly, and she leaned her head against his shoulder.

"No. Just fearful for you in the tournament." That was partly true, at least.

"Don't worry for me." His voice had a tinge of impatience to it and she flinched away, like a dog used to being struck, ready to protect itself from harm. "And don't worry about yourself, either. Once the games are done, I will be One, Ashe will be Two ... and you will be my Three." His tone took on a mischievous lilt, and she turned to him, eager to see him light and happy once more. "Not trapped in a pendant but trapped in my heart."

He took her in his arms and kissed her, and again she felt ... nothing. If he had meant his words to soothe her, they just made her feel claustrophobic.

He fell asleep beside her as he did everything, impatiently and with all his fervour. She lay awake, watching the fire crackling, and the shadows of the maids as they flitted noiselessly about the room. Sten's parting words still echoed in her ears, and she couldn't help turning them over in her mind. 'Ashe won't want Cole's cast-offs.'

What would happen to her if Cole lost?

Cole stirred, and she started, wondering if her thoughts had somehow pierced the fabric of his dreams. He settled quickly with his back to her, and she lay thinking. Ashe wouldn't keep her, she knew that. He'd send her back to ... wherever she had come from. And then what?

She'd be alone, adrift, in a world she could only vaguely remember. The beauty she had come accustomed to, which breathed from every weathered stone and every fragrant flower, every elegant bearing, every ripple of satin cloth as light and shimmering as a butterfly wing, would transform into weather-beaten paint and overgrown cracks in a sidewalk. She wanted to be fae. She wanted to be here. She just wasn't sure if she wanted Cole. If truth be told, she wasn't sure how long she had before Cole didn't want her anymore, either. She had to secure a place of safety that didn't rely on the vagaries of fae whims, but how could she do that if she weren't fae?

She gnawed at a fingernail, the uncertainty of her precarious position making her stomach churn. She sat up and beckoned, whispering to the maid that she'd like something to help her sleep. The maid drew a rose from her pocket, a delicate shade of lilac that appeared dusty brown in the firelight. Ember inhaled the sweet fragrance and lay back against the pillows. Her eyelids grew heavy, and she slept.

CHAPTER 28

S he had almost become accustomed to falling asleep in Cole's room and waking in her own, but there was still that disconcerting sense of displacement when she opened her eyes, of a jigsaw piece being slotted into place as she recognised graceful arched windows that were always open, long white curtains shifting gently in the breeze.

Lily said nothing of her night-time escapades, but she always had a soothing bath ready, brimming with healing oils that calmed the visible marks Cole's passions left upon her. Ever since Ember had given her the gift of glamoured wings, she had been much more open with Ember, chatting about her family who lived down in the nearby village whom she hardly saw since she had taken service in the castle, of her likes and dislikes, and little gossipy titbits about other servants in the castle that made Ember laugh. It surprised her to learn that Ashe's servants weren't just loyal to him, as Cole's were to him, but that they loved him too.

"He was a kind boy," said Lily, soaping a sponge along Ember's shoulders and back during her early morning bath. "But after his cousin Serafina died, he became morose and difficult. He and Cole have always been at odds, but once the tournament is complete, they will become as one, and all will be well."

Ember rose from the tub, her skin glowing from the warm water and from the special oils that left an iridescent shimmer.

"I just want to be quiet today. I'm tired of having to be polite and sweet to all the visiting fae and pretend not to notice when they whisper about me behind their hands: 'look, a human!' It makes me feel like a talking monkey."

Lily suppressed a sly smile. Outraged, Ember threw a towel at her. "I am not!"

Lily laughed. "Perhaps a painting day in the forest? You haven't done that in ages. The other fae won't go in there. It's off limits because of the columns. It would be too easy for someone to enter someone else's kingdom without permission and make mischief."

Ember chewed her bottom lip. The idea was very tempting, but—

"Do you think the prince will let me?"

Lily cast a quick look over her shoulder, a tad dramatic as the two of them were alone, and said in hushed tones, "In my experience, sometimes it's easier to ask for forgiveness than to ask permission."

Ember gave a surprised chuckle. Lily, wings or not, still had a rebellious streak.

Cole might not mind her dragging at his heels all day long, anyway. As the tournament approached, he was becoming increasingly quick-tempered, prone to cutting remarks and cold rejection, although just as quick to lavish extravagant presents upon her; a room filled with roses, a dance choreographed just for her and performed by a hundred fae, another sparkling collar for Rufus. Rufus was almost better dressed than she was.

"We can send a message," said Lily. "Perhaps you can gift him the painting? He might like that."

Ember, Lily and the two assigned guards went to the forest as soon as Lily deemed her fit to be seen in public as the prince's mistress, a person of high standing by tradition. Her dress was immaculate, and she wore diamonds and pearls around her wrists, and dangling from her ears. Lily was however, carrying a shirt she could throw over her gown to protect it from paint spills.

Ember plastered an abstracted smile on her face, nodding politely to those who openly stared at her as she passed them in the halls, and keeping Rufus tucked tightly under her arm because more than one hungry-eyed fae looked as though they might chew him up, diamond collar and all.

When they reached the forest, she told Lily and the guards that she was going to do some painting and she'd rather they weren't breathing over her shoulder as she did so. As a compromise, Lily settled herself against a tree to wait, eyes closed, ankles folded neatly together, while the guards took Rufus for a walk around the forest on patrol. Apart from her bedroom, the forest was the safest place she could be, and in any case, Cole knew where she was.

Ember had her easel set up by the columns, and she swept a single line of green across the canvas, as the beginning of one of the graceful trees that bowed over the Seeds column, the sweeping branches reminiscent of the fern frond carved into the stone. She stared at it for a moment, head tipped to one side, considering, and then took the canvas off the easel and replaced it with a fresh one.

Instead of the scene in front of her, she painted something from memory, something vague and amorphous, of what she could remember of her life before. Smoke, fire, a car upturned, a lonely road, flashing red and blue lights. She painted quickly, the scene not defined sharply, but in blocks and streaks of colour, an impression rather than a replica. The piece had an air of movement and urgency, as though the event had just happened and there was still more to come. As she painted, her memories of the accident became clearer, and she leaned into it, wanting to remember, but it was so difficult, like trying to look through fog.

There came a riffling of a breeze, and she jumped when Ashe said, "Hello."

She took a step back from him, her brush held like a weapon in front of her. "I'm not allowed to talk with you."

Ashe motioned impatiently and there came an almost imperceptible shimmer around them, like the iridescent gloss of a bubble.

"No one will hear us or see us for the moment. We're ... occupying a sliver in time."

She gazed at him, not sure what to say. She hadn't seen him in weeks, ever since the event of the winged horses, and wondered if he knew what Cole had done to her after that, how he'd shouted at her until she cried, and then kissed her tears away, kissed her and caressed her until she had lost herself in a writhing, heated madness.

Ashe looked weary. His face was drawn, and there were shadows under his eyes. Perhaps he'd been sleeping badly too.

"What are you painting?" He moved to see the canvas and inspected it, one finger tapping his lips, his brow furrowed.

She hastened to explain. "It's my parents. The car crash. I remember the air was fresh and icy cold when they dragged me out of the car, but I still couldn't stop coughing."

"And you weren't hurt? Even with the fire?"

"I don't remember. No scars, anyway."

She rubbed her arms convulsively, as if to rid herself of sparks and smuts, and then blinked, letting the present time and day fill her awareness and anchor her again: the green placid trees, the moss beneath her feet, the birds singing high in the canopy.

He was studying her closely, his dark eyes inscrutable, the sharp slash of his mouth softened in the gentle light. "You look tired. I can only assume why."

Her hackles rose at that. "You look tired too. Worse than me. At least I put on make-up to cover it." She fell silent, wondering why it was she always felt the urge to snap at his teasing. She should just let it go. That would probably annoy him more.

"Training has been gruelling," he admitted.

"Perhaps you just need a rest?"

Cole hadn't let such a notion cross his mind; she was sure of it. He would never rest; he would work his team until they were dead from exhaustion. The ceremony for the opening of the tournament was the following day; the pressure was intense.

Ashe gave her an innocent look. "Go to bed, you mean?"

She pressed her lips together reprovingly, although there was a stirring of something in her at the expression in his eyes, not the insta-lust Cole wrung from her drop by drop, but something else. Warm.

"A break. An afternoon somewhere nice and quiet, away from the castle, away from all these visitors. Somewhere you can relax."

"We shouldn't have to socialise as well as train. And yet, they get so offended when you tell them to fuck off."

Ember gave a delighted gasp. "You didn't. Who?"

"The Seeds. Odious creatures. They're constantly at me. Big Cole supporters."

Ember hadn't yet met the rulers of the Seeds, Gered and Samara, but she'd seen them, regal and proud, prowling - for she couldn't think of a better word for the way they moved - around the castle, inspecting the gold vases and graceful statuary with amusement as though they were above such things as decor.

"Where would you go? If you were to have a break?"

There was a mischievous tone to his voice that should have alerted her, but she wasn't listening for it, and in truth, she'd never heard it from Ashe before.

"The beach," she said, promptly. "Where there are no nasties in the water, and everything is sunny and ..."

There came a disconcerting jolt, as though someone had grabbed her and shaken her. She gasped. "Ashe! What have you done?"

CHAPTER 29

P alm trees, swaying in the gentle breeze, white sands curving around out of sight. An aqua blue lagoon, with waters so clear that the tiny fish swimming in the shallows were visible. Further out, a line of white revealing a reef and beyond that the dark blue of the open ocean. Light that was all-encompassing after her days—years, according to Cole—spent in near dark.

The salty air and the crunch of damp sand beneath her toes were enough to convince her this wasn't a dream. And she wasn't in the soft clinging gown she habitually wore in the castle. She was wearing a black string bikini, the triangles barely covering her breasts and bottom. The weight of her necklace had vanished, and she lifted a hand to check, her throat feeling strangely exposed.

She glared at Ashe, and he held up his hands in surrender. The military uniform he wore was gone, replaced with a dark, open shirt revealing a smooth brown chest and lean stomach muscles, and something that looked partly like a loincloth, partly like trunks. Whatever they were, they fitted very well, and she dragged her gaze away before he could catch her staring.

"You said you wanted a holiday," he explained.

She couldn't help a chuckle. "You liar."

"Do you like it, though?"

Yes, she did.

He appraised her frankly, and she tried not to blush at his gaze, not wanting to give him the satisfaction. Instead, she feigned nonchalance and went to the water's edge, dipping her toes in. Without waiting to see what he would do, she splashed in up to her knees and then dove under.

She emerged, spluttering, and called, "No nasties?"

"No nasties," he called back, and she dove under again.

She had a memory of this from her life before, the cool drag against her skin, the lightness of freedom. Although Ashe had suggested she could swim in the lake by the castle, she hadn't wanted to swim with the fae watching her every move. The castle lake was an ominous dark green, thick with lily-pads, and bright crimson flowers, and who knew what lurking below the surface. Here, she was as alone as she'd ever been. She could be herself.

She floated on her back for a time, closing her eyes against the bright sunshine, and then trod water and watched Ashe walking slowly down the beach, hands behind his back, glancing around as though someone was watching him. Even on holiday, it seemed he couldn't fully relax.

When she finally emerged from the water, there were two sand loungers positioned under a straw umbrella a little further up the beach. She sank onto one and reached for the cool drink that had appeared on a nearby table. The cold juice was sweet with the perfect amount of tang, and the soft rush of waves riffling the sand was soothing, lulling her into a state of near zen. She must have slipped into a doze because she startled into wakefulness when Ashe returned and dropped onto the sun lounger next to her. She cracked an eye and smiled.

"Did you enjoy your walk?"

"I did." He sounded surprised. "I don't think that's ever happened before. I just walked up the beach and then kept going. And when I'd had enough, I walked back."

She laughed. "You've never walked before? Like, not to get anywhere, just for the sake of it?"

"Not even then," he assured her gravely.

"And what's around the bend?" She sat up, checking that her bikini top hadn't slipped.

"More of this." He waved an expansive arm. "Just more."

"Is this part of the castle grounds?"

It was definitely fae. Everything was deliberately perfect, every tree as though someone had painted it against the sky, every grain of sand placed just so. The sun was bright and warm but not hot, and even though she'd been in the water for a time without sunblock, her shoulders weren't so much as tinged.

"It's a part of my territory I haven't been before. It lies in a crystal on a table in a hall."

She gaped at him. "We're in ... a crystal?" Like a fortune teller's crystal ball, perhaps. Or a snow-globe, but definitely without the snow.

"I hope nobody knocks it over." He laughed at her wide-eyed look of dismay. "You're safe, Ember."

She wasn't so sure about that. Ever since he'd sat down, there'd been a strange frisson in the air between them. Cole would be furious if he found out that and Ashe had spent the afternoon together. He would rage at her that Ashe was dangerous and not to be trusted, but she wasn't sure if she believed that anymore. Ashe was intense and hard, but he wasn't volatile. She didn't feel that she might set him off at any moment with a wrong word or glance. Being with Cole was like walking a careful line without tripping, ever watchful for a potential pout or frown, and heading it off before it happened, an endless dance to keep a smile on his beautiful face. Ashe was grumpy and morose, but he wasn't spiteful. There was an energy about him that didn't boil and rage but simmered gently somewhere deep within.

"Will he know I'm here?" she asked.

His eye flickered in a wink, the ghost of a smile on his lips. "No."

She stretched, reached for her drink once more. "Then I had better enjoy the peace with all my might."

He considered this and gave a grunt before settling back into his lounger and closing his eyes. She took her drink down to the water, settling on the sand, her toes tickled by the playful little waves that rushed in and back, as though they couldn't make up their minds where they wanted to be. After a time, she plunged back into the water and swam again, delighted by the fish all around her, so unafraid that some of them even let her stroke them, as though they were little water puppies.

When she was tired, she dozed on the lounger, and when she felt hungry, a plate of fruit and cheese appeared. She took a walk around the bend of the beach and saw, as Ashe had said, that the beach continued to curve around the trees, out of sight. She supposed if she kept walking around that long curve, she might end up right back where she started. When she returned, there was an easel and paints set up under a fringed canopy, and she lost herself for a time, painting the sea, sand, and sky.

And all the while, Ashe slept, his stern features relaxed in gentle repose, the lines around his mouth miraculously erased, his brow uncreased for the first time since she'd met him. He looked ... not young exactly, none of the fae she had ever met had looked young. Ageless, yes, but without the innocence and naivete that one normally associated with youth. He looked at peace.

It seemed a long while later before he stirred, mumbling something indistinct, and then he jolted to full wakefulness, reaching automatically to his waist for a weapon—his sword perhaps, or a dagger. After a moment, he dropped his hand and yawned. "I dreamed I was on a tropical island and when I woke, I was on a tropical island, and it was all ... confusing."

She showed him her painting and laughed when he frowned at the abstract picture with broad streaks of blue and dribbles of white.

"What is it?"

He seemed genuinely puzzled, and she gestured around them. "It's here."

"Oh."

"Art isn't necessarily to be understood. Just... experienced."

"Did you like making it?"

"Yes."

"An experience."

"Yes."

"I see."

She wasn't sure if he did, not really, but it didn't matter. "You can have it if you like."

His brows lifted, pleased. "Thank you."

She didn't want to say anything, but the facts were there, nudging at her. The sun hadn't moved from its point in the sky and yet she knew time had passed, a lot of it. She should be back at the castle, waiting for Cole. She could just keep this perfect, peaceful afternoon in a secret crystal tucked in her pocket, and occasionally take it out and marvel at its beauty before she hid it away again.

"I think we should go back."

He didn't say anything, and when she blinked, she was back in the forest by the columns, clad in her flowing gown, diamonds and pearls at her ears and wrists, the press of her collar against her throat.

Her heart sank, and a thrill of foreboding came over her. Lily and the guards had gone, and her abandoned canvas lay on the ground, shredded to ribbons.

CHAPTER 30

U nease pricked at her as she followed a guide back to her room. The hallways were unusually quiet, which only increased her nerves. The floorboards creaked with her every footstep, and from the corner of her eye she fancied she saw shadows shifting and dark fingers reaching for her. She took the last few hallways at a run, her heart pounding, and was relieved when she saw her bedroom door, two guards at attention outside. They opened the door for her without a word, and inside she found Lily restlessly flitting back and forth across the rafters of the ceiling, her glamoured wings shimmering bright in the candlelight, the chandelier swaying from the breeze she created. Rufus worried at a bone in the corner and when he saw Ember, he gave a pleased little snort and a quick wag of his tail, before returning to the far more interesting bone.

"Oh, Ember," Lily cried, flying to Ember, and throwing her arms around her. "I didn't know where you were. I thought perhaps some-one had taken you."

Which, of course, they had.

"I'm sorry. I didn't mean to make you worry. It all happened so fast."

"The prince is ..."

Lily broke off as the door crashed open and Cole burst in, a tornado of smoke whirling about him as though he were in the centre of a storm. He wasn't just angry. He was furious, apoplectic. Ember backed up quickly as he advanced on her, and Lily took her hand as if to give her courage. That sweet little gesture of support was enough to make her stand her ground. She was back now. She was safe.

"Where have you been?"

"In the castle," she answered, a little pertly. "I apologise for making you worry."

"In the castle?" he repeated in an awful mimicry of her, his voice high and quivering, every word laced with derision. "And where, pray tell?"

"I'm not exactly sure."

"You were with him," he snapped. "You were with that foul servant, my Blade. Only one place in the castle I cannot go and that belongs to him, only one place I cannot find you and that is by his side."

She raised her hands in placation, and he slapped them down, and then his hand shot out and he took a handful of her hair, forcing her head back. Her neck cracked and she let out a yelp of pain and terror. He shook her, once, twice, like a dusty mat. Her initial fear turned to anger, and she jerked away from his grasp, pushing Lily behind her.

"Don't touch me," she hissed. "Nothing happened."

"Where were you?" he screamed at her, but she refused to be cowed.

"In a crystal on a table in a hallway," she replied, almost lazily. She was weary of his unpredictable temper, bored with his moods. He wanted her at his side when he felt like it and pushed her away when he didn't, but she wasn't a toy to be thrown aside when he didn't feel like playing with her. It all felt so horribly familiar, and she resented it.

"He didn't lay a finger on me. He was a ..."

She was about to say, a gentleman, but he let out a sharp laugh, one that jangled like rusty springs. "Of course he didn't! The only fae who would bother with a human is me, the only fae who would lower themselves to be with one is me. And what does that say about me? That I'm willing to lie in the filth and the muck? It says that I am not afraid of getting dirty, not averse to consort with the corrupt. I am the most worthy. I am the Sword."

He was panting with his hate, every word laced with venom, but she could see his anger wasn't really about her anymore. It was about Ashe.

"But I'm back now."

She tried to sound as gentle and as soothing as she could, hoping she could dissipate his fury. She'd often foolishly imagined that she had some influence over him, that he respected her. But she saw quite clearly now that no such influence existed. She may have given him some pleasure, but it was of the lowest, most detestable kind. It wasn't two souls connecting in an expression of mutual worship. It wasn't even a joyful act of physical release, for that at least would have been honest and primal and true. Cole was like an addict, pretending he was in control of the drug when, in actual fact, the drug was in control of him. He was with her because he needed her. He drank from her humanity because he had none of his own. And in doing so, it proved to him that he was powerful, untouchable.

Lily plucked at her and whispered, "It's the necklace. That's how he can find you —"

Cole lunged past Ember, seizing Lily in a brutal grip, and hurling her into the air with all his strength. She shot upward, her wings snapping outward. For a moment she hung above Ember, like a guardian angel, and then Cole drew the white sword from his side and slashed once, twice.

Ember shrieked as Lily burst into a thousand million tiny little fragments. Her wings went last, dissolving into a puff of colourful feathers that fell around her like holographic snowflakes. Rufus broke into a howl of terror and flattened himself on the floor. Ember collapsed, her legs refusing to hold her. She gaped up at Cole and scrabbled along the floor until her back pressed against the wall, as far from him as she could get. He covered the space between them in three angry strides, before bending and gripping her chin between fingers of steel.

"You do not defy me. You do not."

He kissed her then, a kiss full of loathing and longing that stole the breath from her lungs and when he pulled away, her lips were bruised, and she could taste blood in her mouth. He vanished, air rushing to fill the empty space. Ember shuddered, her entire body trembling with terror and grief. A single feather drifted across the floor in the gentle breeze and then it too, disappeared.

And Ember wept.

CHAPTER 31

E mber had no memory of going to bed but woke the next morning in a tangle of sheets. Her eyes were sore and felt swollen, and her pillow was damp with tears. A maid was just settling a tray on a table by the window, and for an instant, Ember thought that the night before had just been a hideous, horrible dream. She was about to greet Lily with a cry of relief, but the maid turned, and she saw it wasn't Lily at all, but someone else, a sweet-faced young girl with sharp black eyebrows that winged up at the corners in two straight lines. Her wings were intact too, in mottled shades of brown and black, that Ember had initially mistaken for shadows cast by the flickering candles.

"Good morning," the maid said. "May I get you anything?"

"I don't think so," said Ember. "But the maid who was here last night, Lily, she ..."

"I apologise. I don't know her."

"She has a family, in the village nearby. I should speak to them."

"I don't know them," the maid insisted. "I don't know anything about anyone or anything."

Her pale blue eyes were pleading. She clearly didn't want Ember to push any further, and so Ember gave it up.

She slid out of bed and asked the maid to run her a bath and bring her some clothes. While the maid was occupied, Ember drank a glass of juice and nibbled on a piece of toast smothered with honey. Eating was the last thing she wanted to do, but she needed her strength. She needed to figure out what the hell she was going to do if Cole won. Perhaps it would be best not to wait on the outcome. If she could be gone before the final judgement, then perhaps she had a chance.

She crossed to the window and leaned out. The high wall surrounding the palace grounds was the only thing separating the castle from the greater world of fae. She'd never seen guards patrolling along it, although she assumed they were there, to keep the creatures of the wild at bay.

In the distance, the mountains of the Kingdom of Stones were a pale grey against the darker twilight. Sten might take her in. He'd wanted to buy her. But she didn't want to be owned. She wanted to exist on her own terms. Could she just escape into the wilds and live … where? In the trees? With the spiders?

She thought hard, swallowing automatically, the toast a thick sweet lump that stuck to her teeth. Maybe she should return to her own place on Earth, but that too made her feel uncertain and frightened. She didn't remember enough about it. She couldn't remember where she lived, she couldn't even recall how she'd ended up in Kingdom of Swords. Cole had taken that from her, and she hated him for it.

The bath did nothing to soothe her nerves, and neither did the brushing of her hair or the new dress of silver trimmed in white. The new maid wasn't chatty like Lily. She did everything in silence, and it wore on Ember's nerves. All Ember knew about her was her name, Mira. There came a soft knock at the door and Mira ran to open it, conferring softly with the guard outside before returning with a velvet box.

"The prince has asked you that join him, my lady."

Ember felt panic churn in the pit of her stomach. Would he draw his sword and explode her into a puff of nothing? Her fear must have shown plainly on her face, for the maid was quick to add, "It's the opening ceremony of the Games. The Adjudicator will be there. Everyone will be there." She presented the velvet box to Ember. "A gift from the prince."

Ember regarded it for a second, half-wondering if Cole had put some terrible thing inside, a severed finger perhaps, or some creepy-crawly bite-y creature. She popped the catch, ready to leap back if necessary, and the lid swung open. A beautiful tiara of silver with white opals lay inside. Ember glared at it. "And what's that going to do to me? Track me? Give me hives?"

Mira looked startled. "It's just a decoration. To match your dress."

She removed the tiara from the box and settled it gently on Ember's head, sliding the attached combs into her dark hair so that it wouldn't slip.

Ember went into the bathroom to look at herself in the mirror. Pain and grief were etched plainly on her face, making her eyes liquid and enormous. She could see the collar around her neck easily. It didn't slip in and out of focus from a gold chain to leather. It was all leather now. But the tiara was just a tiara, ostentatious and glamorous, an ornament fit for a princess.

She called Rufus to her and gave him a cuddle before handing him to the maid. "I need you to find him a new home. Somewhere safe."

Tears pricked her eyes, but she blinked them back. The grief she felt now would be minor compared to what she would feel if Cole were to injure or kill him.

Mira took the puppy without question and left the room for a few minutes. She returned empty-handed and when Ember glanced at the corner Rufus preferred, all his things, his basket, his toys, his blanket, were gone too.

She left the room in the company of her new maid and twenty guards, flanked around her with drawn swords. The fae servants in the hallways didn't just move aside, they fairly threw themselves against the wall as she passed, their foreheads pressed against the wood panelling, eyes closed as though they were little children playing hide and seek, hoping that if they couldn't see you, you couldn't see them.

The news of Cole's little performance the night before must have travelled, and she desperately wanted to reach out to one of them, to tell them about Lily and to ask if they could let her family know that she hadn't suffered, that she had just vanished, like a flash of lightning consumed by the night, but the guards didn't slow and she didn't want to get anyone into trouble. So, she just walked on, head held high under the unfamiliar weight of the tiara, wishing the day were already over and she could crawl back into her bed.

They moved in procession outside and into the grounds, and then down a winding path. Cheers and shouts came floating on the breeze, which grew louder and louder, and then they came out of the trees and onto an open flat piece of ground overlooking a deep basin.

Pavilions were arrayed along the lip, all crowded with fae. Ember recognised the water sprites, centaurs, and fairies, but there were many more, some with elongated eyes and scales, others with long tails and pointed ears on top of their heads. At the very front was an empty platform.

The guards led her toward a large white pavilion, and as she came closer, Cole emerged, his hands outstretched, a warm smile on his face. "Darling!" He kissed her, one cheek and then the other, and she closed her eyes as his familiar scent washed over her. She felt the familiar stirring of her automatic response to his presence, but it faded quickly, and she was left with nothing but a bitter taste in her mouth. "I'm so glad you're here."

So that was how he was going to play it? As though nothing had happened at all? Well, she could do that too. She forced a smile, a loving, bright smile, hoping it showed in her eyes, as well as her mouth. "I thank you for the tiara. It's beautiful."

"As are you. Something special for the big day. The greatest of days!"

The fae near him whooped and cheered, and he raised her hand in a celebratory wave. Ember smiled at everyone and tried not to let her lips tremble with the effort.

The guards fell back as Cole drew her into the pavilion, the territory of the Swords, it seemed. All Cole's teammates were there, and she was grateful when Broude squeezed her hand with a glance that said he knew exactly what had happened and felt sorry for it. Lissa was remote and perfunctory in her greetings, but there was a gentleness there too, which surprised Ember. She told Lissa sincerely that she looked very beautiful in her gown of green and silver, and Lissa graciously inclined her head.

A glass of wine was placed in Ember's hand, and she drank deeply, hoping that the alcohol would fog her mind and make this day somewhat more bearable. Cole escorted her to a chair next to some other female fae before leaving to be with his team. The fae didn't exclude her as they normally would, but made an effort to be polite, drawing her into harmless conversation about the wine, the sweets, and the fashions being worn by visiting fae from other kingdoms thronging about the other pavilions. She wondered if there had been some shift in her status, and if her importance had increased in their eyes, or were they just being nice to her because they knew her time was nearly up?

The pavilion next to theirs was their darker twin, and from under her lashes, she saw one of Ashe's teammates, a winged fae who would be challenging Broude in his tournament. She hastily looked away, not wanting Cole to notice that she had even glanced in their direction and caught Lissa staring at her. Ember raised her glass in a mock 'cheers', and Lissa turned away. Her dress was backless and the welts on her back were healing slowly. Clearly, she hadn't used any magical ointments. Perhaps she wanted everyone to see what Cole had done to her. Perhaps she was proud of the marks. Or maybe Cole hadn't allowed her, as a warning to all his court that Cole was at the head and everyone else was his to do with as he pleased.

Ember drained her glass and beckoned a servant for another.

The laughter and chatter abruptly died, and she glanced around to find the cause. It was the Adjudicator, flanked by his jurors, making his way to the very lip of the Basin. The red of their robes stood out like a warning. As he stepped up onto the platform, everyone rose to their feet and Ember followed suit.

The Adjudicator waved a hand, and the flaming tree emerged from the ground behind him, first as a glowing seedling and then a plant proper, and then as the many-branched tree of fire. The pendant glittered from the tree trunk, shadows flitting across the surface. This couldn't be the actual tree, she thought. There was no crackling or hissing, and the Adjudicator didn't look remotely bothered by the heat. As she squinted at it, it flickered like an old TV screen, showing that it was indeed just a glamour, an illusion. The real thing still stood in its place in the castle.

The Adjudicator's voice rang out, unneedful of amplifiers or microphones, a croaking rasp that set Ember's teeth on edge. "The tournament has begun. Three games will determine the winner, and the Sword shall rule with the Blade sheathed at his side."

He beckoned and Cole moved through the crowd, his expression calm and confident. From the other pavilion Ashe emerged, clad in his familiar black, his dark eyes fixed straight ahead. They were both of a similar height, they both walked with their bearing erect and their heads held high. But while Cole tossed smiles left and right to the approving hum of the crowd, Ashe was focused, resolute, ignoring everyone.

They climbed the platform at opposite ends and positioned themselves on either side of the Adjudicator.

"Do you accept the will of the kingdoms?"

"I do," they answered in unison.

"Do you accept the decision of the Adjudicator?"

"I do," they replied, and Ember wondered what would happen if either had said they wouldn't. The Adjudicator didn't look the type to appreciate dissent.

Cole was watching the crowd with a supercilious smile on his face, but Ashe ... Ashe was looking directly at her. He held her gaze for only a moment, but that moment felt like a long, long time. His eyes were dark and luminous, and they held a question— did he hurt you? Her unspoken denial didn't appear to satisfy him, and his eyes narrowed. In that instant, Ember felt both comfort—and fear. If Cole won, she'd have lost the only person in this place who was even vaguely on her side. If Cole won, she was lost forever.

"Then let the tournament begin." The Adjudicator took a step back and held his hands high. The tree blazed bright, and the fae roared their approval. And quick as thought, Cole drew a dagger from his sleeve. His arm lashed out in a roundhouse swing, and he stabbed Ashe in the chest.

CHAPTER 32

Everyone in the pavilion erupted into cheers as Ashe staggered back, his hand at the hilt of Cole's dagger. He looked at it as though he couldn't believe it, and shook his head, plucking the blade out from his ribs and tossing it aside.

There were hisses and boos from Ashe's pavilion and the Adjudicator smiled, a creepy thin-lipped smile that showed broken, yellow teeth. He raised his hands in surrender as if he couldn't possibly intervene and stepped down off the platform. His entourage of jurors closed around him and whisked him away to a blood-red pavilion further along. The tree disappeared. A team of fae dressed in charcoal escorted Ashe away. They cast unfriendly looks and made threatening gestures at Cole's team, who were practically skipping, so jubilant were they at getting in a hit. Guards closed in around their pavilion, as with all the pavilions, the facade of civility gone.

"Well done!" cried Lissa, clapping her hands. Ember glared at her. Now that the tournament had begun, it was clear that the rule about lives being sacrosanct was well and truly over. She couldn't see Ashe for the guards in the way, but she had seen the way his fingers had come away from his side, stained with blood, the look of pain on his face.

Cole strolled past her, and chucked her under the chin, in the manner of a casual caress to a kitten. "Did you see?"

"I saw," she said, forcing a smile.

"The blade was coated with hussop juice," he said with glee. "His healers will be hard pressed to find an antidote before the next game."

"It was admirably done," interjected Lissa. "He'll not heal in a hurry. Pity."

Cole continued walking, making his way through the crowd to the group of centaurs arrayed at the far side. He spoke with them briefly and then clapped Swirl on his muscular shoulder. The team trotted away, breaking into a gallop as they thundered away along the edge of the basin.

Cole sank onto a white velvet padded throne and closed his eyes. Guards came around him, hands on swords, facing outward. A cloud of fog coalesced above his head, surrounding him like a shroud. He had told Ember what would happen during the games, that he would be a conduit of power for his team. He was opening himself, giving them the raw essence of his strength and abilities; his magic would run through their veins. Ashe, in his pavilion, was doing the same, except that Cole had weakened him. He'd suffered blood loss and was probably in terrible pain. This game would be hard on him.

Lissa smiled at Ember. "Congratulations on catching his eye. You gave our prince the opportunity."

A wave of guilt came over Ember, which she disguised with an airy smile, as though mere distraction was what she had intended all along.

Lissa threw her a mocking glance that said she didn't believe that for one second and withdrew into the crowd.

They followed the centaurs out along the ridge, the guards keeping order as they monitored their respective groups of supporters. An obstacle course lay in the chasm below, all tall hedges, rock walls and glistening streams, interspersed with deep pits lined with jagged spears of sparkling rock.

Cole's centaurs made their way along a winding track. Down a facing track, Ashe's team mirrored them. Both teams were clad in colours matching the pavilion canopies, light versus dark, shadow versus sunlight.

The tracks led to opposite sides of the course and when they reached the base, the centaurs rapidly conversed amongst themselves and then spread themselves along each side of the ravine walls, their various weapons: spears, slingshots, bows and arrows, at the ready.

The crowd quietened. Someone shouted, "Team Cole!" and there was a burst of laughter, which soon faded. Ember looked down into the crater, nerves twisting her gut. She wasn't sure of the rules, and from watching the training practises, she wasn't sure if there was much more to it than galloping around the course as fast as you could and to kill those who weren't on your team.

Still, she thought, even if Ashe loses this one, there's two more to go, and it's the best out of three. She crossed her fingers and sent up a wish to whoever was listening. Of the two of them, Ashe was more likely to send her back to Earth, and even if he didn't, perhaps he'd just let her live her life, tucked away in a corner of the castle, free to paint and dream. It would be a lonely sort of life, she argued with herself. No family, no friends, no ambition, nothing to pursue, nothing to strive for, no one to share it with.

Or perhaps Ashe would remember that she had distracted him at the worst possible moment. She was the only human in this strange place. Maybe Ashe would put her in a zoo, she thought with a bleak attempt at humour. Let the fae stare and throw food at her. He might put her in a dungeon and leave her there until she starved to death. Or perhaps he'd decide she was too much to deal with and explode her like Lily.

She fisted her hands, concealing them amongst the folds of her dress. Her future was too uncertain here. She wished she'd asked Ashe what he would do to her if he won. She should have. She'd been too busy enjoying her holiday on the beach.

A gong sounded, a reverberating crash that echoed around the canyon, and on cue, radiating lines of white light came shooting out from Cole's pavilion, criss-crossing through the air, looking like a spider-web designed by a drunk spider, shooting down and down to the waiting centaurs.

The light pierced them, and they arched their backs, rearing up onto their hind legs, heads flung back with mouths open in either agony or ecstasy. Ember couldn't tell which, but knowing Cole, it was probably both.

On the other side of the canyon, black streamers of light met Ashe's team, but the black light wasn't as strong or defined as the white. The white was a sharp line of lightning that cut across the ravine, the black was like smoke, insubstantial, wavering.

Both teams froze in place, suffused in the power of the princes, and then the webs of light vanished, and the game was on.

She watched with unseeing eyes as the centaurs tore back and forth, shouting instructions and insults. Three went down quickly, two from Ashe's team with arrows bristling from their sides, the other from Cole's team, draped across an outcrop of rocks with a caved-in skull.

It was soon clear that Cole's team had the upper hand. They were that much faster, that much more accurate with their weapons. One after another, Ashe's team fell. Tinth, their leader seemed to be everywhere, whirling a deadly spiked ball on a chain in one hand, chasing down opponents, felling them and then trampling them under his massive hooves. But it wasn't enough. When Tinth took a spear from Swirl, tumbling into one of the deadly pits, the rest of the team lost heart and the aftermath was bloody and brutal.

Ember cheered along with the rest, although the sight of the slain sickened her, and as the fae retired to their pavilions, both Cole and Ashe were carried back to the castle on litters, eyes closed, faces pale. When the guards came to escort her back to her room, she was dangerously tipsy from several swift glasses of wine, and with a feeling of relief, she thought Cole would have no further use for her that day. But to her dismay, she was told she needed to get ready. The first ball of the tournament was in a matter of hours, and he expected her to be there.

CHAPTER 33

The dress Mira brought out was a confectionery of gossamer layers in cream and gold, with a heart-shaped neckline, a nipped-in waist, and several layers of layers of netting under a silk skirt. The material flounced out wide, making it appear as though she were gliding across the floor. The ball was a masquerade, and she wore a mask designed like a white butterfly with outstretched wings. Her mask covered her head, dropping to cover both eyes and her nose, but left her lips and cheeks bare apart from a dusting of gold powder that accentuated her cheekbones. She wore opalescent silk gloves up to her elbows and her black hair loose down her back, and when she looked in the mirror, she thought she looked like some kind of gorgeous metallic insect, vaguely threatening, aloof and inhuman.

The masquerade, she learned, was another tradition. Both teams were in attendance, and the masks helped to give a veneer of protection. If nobody knew who anyone was, they were safe from harm.

It was a silly fancy, she thought. Anyone would recognise Cole or Ashe from their bearing alone, but she said nothing. When she had first arrived in the Kingdom of the Swords, she had been blithely unaware of how precarious her existence was, determined purely on Cole's whim. She'd acted like a privileged tourist in a foreign country, gaping at this and that, asking inappropriate questions, accepting the presents, the food, the satisfaction of every want, as though it were hers by right.

Now she felt as though everything she did was being held in judgement of her. Every inane comment she made would be used against her later, every mistake was evidence, every thoughtless remark a weapon. She had to be careful. She had to tread lightly. And so, she sat quietly while Mira painted her face and adjusted her dress, and she made no protest when it was time to go with the guards.

She'd been down these corridors before. They were the ones lined with cold stone, the ones that led to the hall where the tree grew. And when the guard flung open the door, she saw she was right, although the hall looked different, decorated in bronze and gold, and extended to accommodate the hundreds of fae inside. A wall of ice, sculpted into fantastical figures, stood against the tree's fire, keeping the temperature in the hall comfortable, and clouds of steam rose from the icy blocks. The sight was even more dazzling than the gorgeous costumes the fae wore. Ember had to stand on tiptoe to glimpse the pendant set into the trunk, the dangling chain jerking and twisting as if Tana the Blade could hear the music and wanted to get out.

"A dance, little stranger?" said a voice, and she turned to see a horse's head bending down toward her. The fabulous mask covered his face, towering high, and yet, she would have known his wings anywhere.

"Broude!" she said warmly and then clapped a hand over her mouth as he shook his head sternly at her, his mane flicking from side to side. "Sorry. I mean, handsome horse-man, I would love to dance."

She didn't want to, not really. She didn't want to be swallowed up in this unpredictable mob replete with glamour and danger, but she couldn't refuse, either.

Broude took her in his arms and as the music swelled, she let him sweep her away into a riotous whirl of leaping and gyrating and rising into the air. At the end of the dance, she was laughing and breathless, and then someone else took her hand and propelled her into another dance, and she lost herself twirling around and around the tree.

It wasn't so awful after all, she decided. The other kingdoms were all there, vying to outdo one another with towering headdresses, outrageous costumes, and elaborate masks. Her inhibitions faded with every glass she drank, and she danced with fae after fae: some with wings, some without, some with tails or scales or fangs or spikes, others insubstantial as mist. And eventually she was intoxicated enough that she felt she could be herself, the traditional masks giving her a semblance of anonymity.

She danced with Sten who knew exactly who she was, and who whispered in her ear that all she had to do was say the word and he'd take her away, and she laughed and spun away from him, because who could say what would happen to her in the Kingdom of the Stones? Better the fae you know than the fae you don't, she reasoned.

She danced until she was dizzy, and when she stumbled, a powerful arm caught her, drawing her close. A pair of dark eyes gazed at her from a charcoal mask fashioned like a wolf's head studded with lustrous black pearls, the mouth set in a familiar stern line.

She cast a sweeping look around for Cole, but couldn't see anyone in particular for the crush of fae around her, and so she pulled her courage together and whispered, "Are you alright?"

"Better than I was," came the dry reply. "And you?"

"He was very angry."

She couldn't tell him the rest, about poor little Lily, because the words seemed to stick fast in her throat, and she had to be quick because she didn't know who was watching, who was listening, who might report back to Cole and tell him that his little pet was dancing with his greatest rival. Instead, she said in a voice barely more than a whisper, "Promise to send me back if you can."

He gave a low chuckle with no mirth in it. "Finally thinking of your own precious hide? Slow, aren't you?"

"Not as slow as you," she snapped. "You could have dodged."

He gave a chuckle at that, and she relented. "I think it was a cruel trick, if you must know."

"Really?" He eyed her with curiosity, his mouth curved in disbelief. "It was well within the rules."

"Rules don't matter here. Just power."

He spun her out and back again. "You want to leave all this?" His tone was mocking, and the flames of the tree were reflected in his eyes, dancing gold and bronze, a fire lighting up the darkness.

The glitter and glamour, the violence and clamour ... yes, she was ready to leave it all. "Promise me."

He didn't answer, just spun her out again and their fingers broke apart. Off balance, a dancing couple jostled her, and when she was steady on her feet again, Ashe was nowhere to be seen.

She moved to the edge of the hall to rest upon a couch and met a couple of fae from the Kingdom of Sands. They were intrigued by her, but as custom dictated at the masquerade, didn't probe too closely as to her true identity. They knew who she was though, for they asked if she'd ever been beyond the Kingdom of Swords' borders.

"There's more to Esha than this little place," one of the fae said. Her dark skin glittered with gold flecks, and she wore loose flowing pants that caught at the ankle, with two bands criss-crossed over her breasts. Gold bangles jingled with every gesture and her mask was more like a veil, a gauzy kerchief that fluttered with her breath as she talked. "The Kingdom of Sands is the most refined, truly. None of this ugly stone and those weedy gardens. Every wall of the Sands palace looks like lace, every floor is a mosaic of jewels and colour, every tree and flower placed to delight the eye. You should visit."

"I'm not sure I'm allowed," Ember murmured, a little dazzled by her companions. They were very beautiful and had an air of confidence that made her feel lonely and small. Had she always felt like this? She couldn't remember.

"Then you must make a pilgrimage to the pit instead. It's at the heart of the kingdom. Surely they'll allow you that? It's history, after all. Educational! The fire-pit holds the Treaty of the Swords inside. I mean, you can't see it or anything. Because of all the flames, you know. But with all the temples around it, it's quite a sight."

The fae next to her shuddered delicately. "What's with the Swords and all the fire, anyway?" she complained. "Candles everywhere, that ridiculous tree. It's barbaric. The only fire that matters is the sun."

She stretched out her arms skyward, upturning her face to the heavens, and a secondary pair of arms that Ember hadn't noticed unfolded themselves from her back and stretched, too.

"I suppose because swords are forged in fire?" Ember volunteered tentatively.

The fae looked at her in surprise and nodded. "That makes sense."

"Isn't she clever?" came a voice. Cole's mask was elaborate and fanciful, a tree rising high above his forehead in mimicry of the tree of fire, although his was bedecked with white roses, and clouds of sparkling fairies hovered about the flowers.

The Sands' fae quickly made their excuses and departed, apparently recognising him as easily as Ember had. He held out a hand, and she clasped his fingers lightly, rising to her feet. "And you're right, you know. Fire is the birthplace of the Swords. Fire cleanses us all."

He took Ember in his arms and nuzzled her neck, making the hairs on her arms stand up, not in pleasure or desire, but in wary apprehension. He led her out onto the floor for a dance, a slow one, and she pressed her body against his and gave every impression of a woman in love—she sighed, she smiled, she trailed her fingers along his shoulder, she closed her eyes in rapturous delight, but inside, she felt as cold and grey as the stone walls of the castle.

Over his shoulder, she caught sight of a dark gaze from behind a black pearl-studded mask, and then as Cole turned her around in a slow twirl, she fixed her eyes on the orange jewelled pendant nestled in the tree, the dark shadows within flickering back and forth, back and forth.

Chapter 34

The ball ended at the stroke of midnight, but many had left well before then, not wanting to be caught up in a tussle between the two teams. Cole's stabbing of Ashe had been the gossip of the ball, and all supposed that Ashe would have to retaliate soon, out of honour and shame.

The ball may have been off limits for violence, but all that ended when the clock struck twelve. When the teams vanished early from the hall, the fae became even more wild and raucous, the simple rebellion of school children whose teachers had left the classroom. Fae from the different kingdoms were engaged in passionate clinches all over the hall, and the dancing was lascivious and wanton. Clothing lay discarded on the floor trampled by uncaring feet, and everywhere Ember turned, fae were kissing, groping, touching, and enjoying each other.

The wine had caused several to pass out cold, and there were arguments too, and physical fights. A fae from the Stones beat a fae from the Seeds into a bloody mess before throwing him high over the ice wall into the tree. His shrieks as the fire consumed him were horrible, but the dancing didn't slow, and the rulers of the Stones and Seeds just shrugged and snapped their fingers for more wine.

Ember left the hall after that, shaky from watching the fae burn, a strange memory of meat sizzling on a black street nudging at her mind.

She showered when she returned to her room, cleansing herself of gold dust, spilled wine, and perspiration, and then slipped between cool sheets with a sigh.

"Sleep well," Mira said as she left. "The Winged Eagles take flight tomorrow."

"Already?"

"The Adjudicator has decided. We leave early. The game will take hours."

The second game and the Adjudicator had allowed hardly any time for Ashe to recover from his wound. Did that mean then, that he was secretly on Cole's side?

Ember fell asleep quickly, tired from the day, but her dreams were twisted and strange. Broude mounted on a stallion of fire, scooping her up as he galloped past. As she struggled to get free, he let her drop, down, down, down through the clouds, down into a pit of fire... she woke with a cry, covered with a light sheen of sweat, her hands twisted in the sheets.

Sleep was elusive and her stomach felt queasy after all the wine from the night before, and so she lay staring at the ceiling, a myriad of images marching through her head: the pendant, the tree, Lily exploding into dust, the mirror that showed her home - the mirror, if what Ashe had said so long ago was correct, that had first shown her to Cole. She lay, thinking and thinking, and then it was morning, and Mira came in with a breakfast tray and a medicated draught to settle her hangover.

A short time later, the guards escorted her to a gilded carriage pulled by two midnight black horses. Mira pointed out a range of rugged hills behind the castle, their destination for the second tournament. The maid settled inside with her, folding her wings in tight, while the guards got into formation on horseback, to the front and rear of the carriage.

It was the first time Ember had left the castle grounds, and she gazed out the window with interest. The land here had been settled by the common folk for ages upon ages, the maid told her, and the pastures were smooth rolling green, with sweet little thatched cottages dotted here and there, thick with climbing roses and honeysuckle. There were fields of herbs and vegetables, and plenty of grazing for cows, sheep, and goats. Tiny fairies swarmed the hedgerows, and toads as big as small children wandered about on two legs, dressed in tiny waistcoats and trousers, making Ember cover her mouth with a gasp, ducking behind the carriage curtain for fear they would take offence at her laughing at them. The toads were in charge of the waterways and ponds and held quite a high standing in the kingdom.

It all looked mellow and peaceful, but Mira assured her that danger lurked here, too. There were poisonous plants that could kill at a touch, and massive tawny birds flying overhead, with hooked beaks and sharp claws, which made the guards draw their bows and arrows lest the birds swoop down and carry them off. Fearsome beasties lurked in the pockets of wild forest, eager to snatch an unwary traveller, and there were other fae too, untamed and hostile.

Their destination wasn't far as the crow flies, but the road twisted and turned, adding extra time to the journey. The road soon climbed uphill, and the horses strained as they hauled the carriage up over the rutted, stony tracks. Soon Ember was told to climb out, that she'd have to walk the rest of the way. She didn't mind that so much— the carriage was beautiful and the cushions very luxurious, but it had been a bumpy ride, and her stomach was in no mood for it.

She held her skirts in one hand and followed the other fae up the track, wishing her shoes were a little more substantial than thin-soled satin. Mira, noticing Ember stumble over rocks and clods of earth, told a guard to carry her, and ignoring Ember's protests, the guard lifted her into his arms as though she were a sleepy child. She closed her eyes in embarrassment, the metal studs of his uniform digging into her side and causing her nearly as much discomfort as her shoes.

Eventually, they came to the white pavilion set up on a bluff over-looking a vast valley below. A black pavilion stood on the opposite side of the valley, so far away that it was impossible to make out anyone in particular. The ravine wasn't the placid, gentle dip of the gully at the training grounds. Jagged scars from rockfall pocked the steep sides, heaped rubble lined the base of the ravine, far below. Already ensconced in his throne at the far end of the tent, Cole sat, eyes closed, fingers resting lightly in his lap. A pulsating cloud surrounded him, presumably about to burst forth in a web of white lightning.

Broude and the rest of his Winged Eagles waited along the edge of the bluff. The horses were gleaming, perfectly groomed, stamping and tossing their heads, in an impatience to be off, and the fae who rode them were eager and alert, checking bowstrings and pannier straps. Peaks lay all around, each with an apple tree growing on top, each loaded with golden apples that twinkled in the light. The game was simple. A point per apple, and the team with the most apples won.

Ember approached the throne, wondering if Cole was too focused on his team to notice she had arrived, but he opened his eyes as she drew close and the guards surrounding him let her through. The thick mist drifted and whispered about him, and she had a fancy that it was coiling about to look at her.

"Darling." His voice was faint and far away, as though he was somewhere else. "How exquisite you are."

"I came to wish you good fortune, Your Highness." She gave as graceful a curtsey as she could manage.

He smiled, and she wondered if his teeth had always been that sharp, if his features had always been so narrow and pointed, like a white rat, and she immediately banished the thought from her mind lest he could somehow read it.

"I hear you danced with my cousin last night," he said, and she blanched.

"Did I? I had no idea! With all the masks and things." Her voice sounded nervous and unconvincing to her own ears, and she hoped Cole would take it as confusion for accidentally consorting with the enemy rather than a deliberate choice. "How dare he! He is utterly without honour. He knows I belong to you." She stroked her collar, giving him a glowing look from under her lashes, hoping to distract him.

The mist took on a grey tinge, writhing about him, and he smiled. "I've missed you. When the games are over, I shall devote all my energies to you."

"I look forward to it," she said, and watched dispassionately as his smile grew wider.

"Away with you, kitten. I can't possibly concentrate with you looking so ... appealing."

She swept another curtsey and sauntered away into the crowd, wondering if he was watching her, but when she snuck a look back, his eyes were closed, his guards back in position to prevent anyone else coming close.

She let out a shuddering sigh and started as a hand clamped onto her shoulder. Lissa was glaring at her. "Quite the little performance."

"I have no idea what you're talking about."

Ember's heart was still thudding in her chest, her hands clammy. Lissa's barbs were nothing compared to her relief at discovering that although Cole knew she'd danced with Ashe, he was apparently unaware she'd also begged Ashe to take her away.

"Shouldn't you be with the rest of your teammates? Cheering them on and whatnot?"

Lissa gave an irritated huff. "I'm sick to the back teeth of all of them. We've been in each other's pockets for weeks, months. After our match is done, I swear I'll not so much as speak to any of them ever again."

It amused Ember to see Lissa dropping her guard. Perhaps she and Lissa had reached some kind of understanding. They were both lovers of the prince, and both had suffered under his hand. That gave them something in common. They might even be friends.

"You're nervous?"

Lissa raised an eyebrow. "How human of you. Fae would never ask that."

Ember frowned. Perhaps not. "I apologise if I offended."

"I am ..." Lissa paused, thinking, and finally said, "I am eager to be done with the games. Eager to see the back of the Adjudicator and all his little red sycophants. And proud to serve the Sword afterwards. The prince has said I might take on a greater role in his rule."

"Like ... on a council or something?"

Ember wasn't sure if the Kingdom actually had a council. So far, she'd only seen Cole rule, with everyone else scurrying to do his bidding. His voice was their voice. His whim was their pleasure to serve. A dictatorship.

"Esha isn't the only world served by the Sword."

Lissa's smile was sly, and with a faint incline of her head, she slipped away into the crowd, leaving Ember to wonder what she meant.

The gong sounded with a crash, and the fae roared in anticipation, surging to the front of the pavilion. The white shroud around Cole spread like a blob of watercolours being blown by a straw into spidery lines shooting through the roof and toward the winged fae and their horses.

Everyone was occupied. Everyone was in thrall to the game.

Everyone except Ember.

CHAPTER 35

T he Winged Eagles were like predatory demons, soaring and diving through the air as the riders collected golden apples from the trees. The sky was thick with arrows and one by one, both horses and riders were struck, tumbling helplessly into the ravine below.

There were fights in midair, with horses biting and kicking, their great wings colliding together with great smacking sounds, as the mounted fae slashed at each other with swords. Blood streamed down glossy necks and shining flanks, and apples spilled from the panniers like beads from a broken necklace.

The game went on for what seemed like hours, and eventually Broude fell, two arrows piercing his torso, his horse lifeless from a sword through the neck. Ember's eyes filled with tears, her throat tight with grief, remembering how they had danced and laughed together, how safe she had felt in his muscular arms.

It was Ashe's team who was ultimately victorious. The remaining flyers landed on the other side of the valley, horses with heaving sides flecked with sweat, fae bowed with broken wings, surrounded by a web of black that was so thick and viscous, it looked like spilled ink.

A rapturous applause came from their pavilion, the cheers carrying on the breeze across the valley to Cole's supporters. They stood dumbfounded in their silence, hands covering mouths in shock.

Cole had sagged across the throne, eyes closed, his face white, a tracing of black veins clearly visible under his skin, tracking across his flesh like scribbles from a pen. Fae healers attended him, ordering the guards to get him back to the castle at once. Lissa, hovering nearby, had to be restrained from going with him and in her fury struck a guard across the face. Seeing Ember, she whirled and advanced on her.

"I suppose you're happy now?"

Ember took a step back. Clearly, the unspoken truce was over.

"Don't be ridiculous. I feel awful."

"He needs your support, even if you are on the other side."

"I'm not, and I know."

Ember was getting cross now. More than one fae was staring at them curiously, and she had no desire to be accused of being disloyal to the prince. "I'll do anything for His Highness, you know that," adding with a faint smile, "but I'm not that good a rider."

Lissa stared at her and then laughed. "I suppose not. You would have been the first at the bottom of the ravine." She gnawed at a knuckle and muttered, "After everything he did to become heir and now this. It's payback. Serafina's revenge."

Ember frowned. "What?"

"Never mind. Get back to the castle. And here's a fair warning. Don't leave your room. It'll be dangerous in the halls tonight."

"When isn't it?" Ember called after her as Lissa disappeared into the crowd streaming back through the pavilion. They were eager to leave, shoving past Ember on all sides. She finally emerged from the pavilion, skirts askew and hair dishevelled, to find Mira waiting for her, stark relief illuminating her face.

"Where have you been?" Her usually melodious voice was fretful, and she took Ember by the elbow, steadying her over the rutted earth.

"I was at the far end of the pavilion. It was a terrible thing to see."

The guards closed around them and one of them made to scoop Ember up and carry her down the rocky path.

"I'm fine." Ember tried to wave him off, but he bent and swept her up anyway, and she gritted her teeth, settling in for a bumpy trip.

There was none of the gaiety and artless chatter of the way up. The fae moved in utter silence, heads bowed. At the head of the trail, they climbed into waiting carriages, mounted their horses, or leapt into the air and flew back to the castle.

Even the castle itself looked to be in mourning. Cole's hallways were dark and dank, and black, clammy fog swirled across the floorboards. Candles winked out, impossible to light, and the soft twilight had become a gloomy dusk, the light a steel grey that made everything feel cold and miserable. In the darkest corners, creatures emerged from the cracks in the walls, creatures that hissed, scurried, and snapped as one hastened past, creatures with yellow eyes and sharp teeth and a taste for flesh.

It was a hurried trip back to her room and when they got there, Mira closed the door and locked it. The fairies who usually swarmed the flowers at the windowsill had disappeared, and Mira closed the windows for the first time since Ember had arrived, drawing the curtains. Mira tried to light a fire in the fireplace to chase the chill away, but it smoked and spluttered as though the wood was wet inside, and in the end, Ember crawled into bed while the maid settled on the trundle beside her. Ember pulled the covers over her heads, trying not to hear the scratching and scrabbling of the dark things scuttling behind the flagstones of the walls, and she dozed uncomfortably until the morning.

The next day, the shadows had marginally lifted, but the atmosphere was still gloomy. Mira, who had briefly left the room for Ember's breakfast tray, reported that Ashe had held a grand ball the night before to celebrate his win. The dancing was still going strong, and not expected to cease until nightfall.

The Adjudicator had announced that the third and final game was to be held in three days' time. Lissa's team would tackle the obstacle course in the water, and then, Ember thought, her fate would be decided.

She wished she had the distraction of a ball to dance her worries away. It didn't seem quite Ashe's style somehow. Most likely, he had thrown the ball for his team and supporters, rather than for himself. He wasn't like Cole, who needed to be surrounded by servants, sycophants and entertainments every moment of the day, the subject of adoring eyes and animated gossip. In fact, she thought with wry amusement, a glamorous party to which he was uninvited would likely needle Cole more than anything else.

After a day with little more to do than pace her bedroom floor, she told Mira she'd like to go to the forest to paint. Mira suggested she paint in her rooms, but Ember protested that the forest had better light. Mira extracted a promise from Ember to always stay in the company of her guards - no slipping off anywhere. Ember agreed, and she readied herself for a quick trip through the castle, the guards with their daggers drawn ready to stab any scuttling creepie that dared attack.

They had almost made it to the forest when the guard at the lead of their little procession slowed, his head tilted to look up at the wall. Ember followed his gaze. There was nothing there, just a black crack between the wooden beams ... and then the crack fell off the wall, and she realised it was a snake, a long, hissing black snake, whipping through the air. The guards thrust Ember back, and the snake flew past her, settling around Mira's neck.

Mira gasped, sucking in a choking breath as the coils tightened around her throat, and then the snake reared up and sank sharp fangs into her cheek. The guards raised their blades and hesitated, not wanting to stab it lest they get the maid instead. Finally, one lunged forward, seizing the snake behind the head. It hissed in fury, and the guard yanked. The body loosened and fell away.

Mira slumped, and the guard threw the snake to the floor. Another stomped on it with a heavy boot, and then bent and stabbed it with a dagger. Black blood sprayed, spattering the floorboards. Ember rushed to Mira, easing her sagging body to the ground. Mira's cheek was swelling rapidly, her breathing raspy and laboured. After what had happened to Lily, Ember couldn't bear the thought of another maid coming to grief in her service.

"She needs a healer."

The guard looked at Ember for what seemed like the first time, and his voice had a tinge of respect in it. "A healer? For a servant?"

"Do you know of one?"

"Of course."

"Then take her, please."

"As you wish, my lady."

The guard cradled Mira in his arms, and set off at pace, another guard at his heels. Even armed and armoured, the guards were loath to walk alone. Ember watched them go, and then, disinclined to return to her gloomy rooms, carried on to the forest.

The trees felt safer than the dark hallways, the soft light comforting and warm. Ember wondered if Alena had anything to do with that. She decided to have her easel and paints set up next to the pond, so she could call on the water fae if need be. The guards arranged themselves in a semicircle around her, and Ember began to paint.

She tried to replicate the intricate grooves of a gnarled tree trunk but couldn't settle to it, and then she turned her hand to reproducing a sweet collection of flowers sticking up from a clump of moss, but she wasn't happy with that either.

Finally, she painted a dress she had seen a fae wearing at the masquerade, a gorgeous concoction of muted sunset colours and layers. Steadily the picture grew to include a gathering of fae dancing, laughing, and enjoying themselves, as free as the music they were dancing to, a whirl of colour and light. In the middle, another figure emerged, a shadow of stern darkness amongst the gaiety and charm of the rest, two dark eyes gazing out to meet hers.

She stepped back from the canvas, flexing her cramped fingers, and almost dropped the brush in fright when Lissa emerged from the trees.

"What are you doing here?" She'd never imagined the perfectly groomed Lissa as the type to enjoy the great outdoors - even if the outdoors was, well, indoors.

"I was told to come and check on you." There was a taut anger to her tone, that of a lady being ordered to do a servant's work. She looked at Ember's picture and her eyes narrowed. When she finally looked up, her beautiful face was aghast. "After everything the prince does for you, you prefer this?"

She jabbed a finger at the canvas, at the figure of Ashe staring at them, and then she lost all reason, slashing at it with sharp fingernails that had become like claws. Ashe's painted eyes shredded, and she flung the remains of the canvas to the forest floor. "All the time you've been mooning after him, that depraved, lying beast ..."

In a fury, she slapped Ember across the face, sending her flying to the ground. Her face felt as though it had grown to twice its size, and Lissa's voice sounded as if it was coming from very far away. "Stand down," she was shrieking at the guards. "Stand down!"

She held more status and power in the castle than Ember, and none of the guards moved a muscle as Lissa viciously kicked her in the ribs. The wind was knocked out of her, and she gagged, trying to draw a full breath, but Lissa kicked her again, screaming, "Traitor! Filth!"

"Stop," Ember tried to say, but nothing came out. She rolled away, staggering to her feet, and clutched blindly at her equipment table. She seized a palette knife and brandished it weakly.

Lissa laughed with derision. "What are you going to do, paint me to death?"

As Lissa took aim with a balled-up fist, Ember slashed out at her, catching her across the wrist. Lissa shrieked in surprise, although the knife's edge was blunt, and at most, had merely scratched her.

"You saw!" she shrieked at the guards, utterly undone. "You all saw she drew a weapon on me!"

She had lost all reason, deep within the grip of a jealous madness. She seized Ember, her hands tangled in Ember's hair, and dragged her over to the pool. Lissa threw her down and forced Ember's head under the water. Ember struggled and fought, but Lissa's grip was firm. Black spots danced in her vision; she was growing weaker by the second ...

A face appeared in front of hers and she blinked, trying to focus, but she couldn't see much, other than two eyes, like sparkling sapphires. The face vanished and the grip on her scalp abruptly ceased. She dragged herself from the water, coughing and spluttering, retching with pain and shock, and then eyes widened, her mouth dropping in horror.

The forest was fighting back. A carpet of moss crawled up Lissa's and the guard's legs, trapping them in place. They tried to yank their legs free, but it was hopeless. They were caught as if in quicksand.

Vines swung down from the canopy, entwining them in knotted ropes, and Lissa screamed and then gagged as a thick vine coiled around her neck. Her face turned a livid purple as she scrabbled helplessly at the plant, as all the while the moss crept up and up her body. A guard on his knees was almost completely smothered, a living statue of soft green.

Trees creaked and cracked, swinging heavy branches, ripping at armour and tearing at flesh. Ember scrabbled back, but the forest paid no attention to her. When the last guard had drawn his last breath, the trees flexed themselves as if stretching sore muscles, and then settled back to their original, silent splendour. Moss completely covered the bodies, and the only clue they were there was a glint of silver armour here and there, a lock of pale hair peeking through the green. A sigh rose from the forest that seemed to come from every living being, and then there was nothing but the sound of birdsong throughout the canopy.

CHAPTER 36

S trength depleted, Ember fell back onto the moss, her breathing ragged and tired. She thought she might have cracked one of her ribs in the vicious beating she had endured. Half-dazed, she thought she heard a rushing of wind through branches and wondered if the forest had come to life again to swallow her up. Surprisingly, she found she didn't care at all. The rustling noises separated themselves into a babble of voices and a horrified screeching. Something grabbed her and jerked her to her feet. She cried out in pain, and then her knees collapsed.

There was no guard safely cradling her in his arms now. Two guards on either side forced her through the forest, yanking her to her feet every time she stumbled, hustling her without mercy. She sobbed under her breath, wanting to wipe her streaming nose, but they had her arms in too firm a grip, and she couldn't. Along the corridors they went as passing fae stared and whispered.

They dragged her through a doorway and forced down onto her knees. She looked up, tangled hair dripping around her face, eyes streaming with pain and humiliation.

Cole sat on his throne, his face drawn and paler than usual. He looked diminished somehow. Rage and disgust oozed from every pore, and the grey shadow around him pulsed and vibrated ominously.

"What have you done?" he said, his voice barely controlled.

For an instant she thought he was referring to her painting of Ashe, but he surged to his feet and shouted, "You have murdered my champion!"

The unfair accusation straightened her spine, and she looked him full in the face. "I did not."

"You have killed her, my Lissa, my chance, my rulership, you have killed her, you have killed her for him!"

He was incoherent, gibbering in his rage, and the shadow gathered force, billowing forward to engulf her. She choked on it as it surrounded her, but apart from the smell, like rancid clothing and wet rotting food, it didn't hurt. She'd expected her flesh to peel back, her bones to crumble, but there was nothing.

It withdrew, and with its absence, she became aware of another presence standing beside her. Alena. She looked as matronly as ever, clad in her usual shimmering green, her skin glistening as though wet, but there was a heat rolling from her, a tangible aura that Ember recognised as power, in its most base, true form. Alena held as much power as the princes, Ember realised, perhaps more. She was smiling, yes, but there was a savage glint in her eye, and Ember was profoundly glad that it wasn't directed at her.

Cole was shaking, his mouth working, clearly attempting to control himself. The mist had withdrawn to hover about him, somewhat lessened than before, more white than grey.

He drew a deep breath. "Alena. This is no business of yours."

"Your information is incorrect," said Alena in the smooth, vaguely dismissive tone that Ember knew so well. She gave Ember a fleeting glance and in it, Ember saw the shadow of a wink. "This is more my business than anyone else's. It occurred in my rooms, after all."

"This ... human ... murdered my champion. She has destroyed any chance I have of winning the tournament. Teams must be complete. I will be the Blade by default! I have lost! And she was his hand."

"Your Highness," said Alena.

Her tone was icy, reproving, and Cole sank back into his throne, a white knuckled grip on the throne's arms, as if they were the only thing preventing him from launching into a physical attack.

"This human did nothing. The castle itself murdered your champion in defence of the innocent. Are you to defy its decision? Might I remind Your Highness that you are here at the castle's discretion. Your presence is by permission, not by right."

Ember didn't know what to make of this. The castle was its own entity, and the princes lived here because it chose to let them? She tucked that nugget of information away as Alena continued.

"Under these ... exceptional circumstances, I suggest you make a case to the Adjudicator."

Cole looked poleaxed. Ember could almost see his mind working. "Then there is a chance."

"There is always a chance." She took Ember's hand, raising her to her feet. "The girl is hurt. She suffered at the hands of the water sprite. She needs a healer."

Cole gave a brief nod, and a fae appeared at Ember's side. Alena gently caressed Ember's hair, her touch fading as she dissolved into nothing. The fae bore Ember away, and Cole didn't utter a word.

She was glad to see Mira back in her rooms. A light bandage covered her cheek, and although she looked wan and shaky, she sprang into action as soon as the fae brought Ember in, making sure she was comfortable on the bed and then helping the healer to apply salves to her bruises.

The healer laid her hands on Ember's sore ribs and closed her eyes. A tingling began under her fingertips, an icy tingle that flowed through Ember's body, swirling around her midriff before dissipating throughout the rest of her, as clean and refreshing as a mountain stream. She took a breath, and then another, deeper, her ribs no longer hurting.

They helped her to sit, and she gave them both a grateful smile, but to her surprise, neither smiled back. Both were uneasy, and the healer hurried to the door as soon as she was able, leaving Mira to needlessly fluff up the already fluffed up pillows on the couch.

"I'm sorry," Ember said, although she didn't know if she was or not. Lissa had brought her retribution on herself, and she couldn't help it if the trees had killed Lissa in Ember's defence.

"It isn't your fault, my lady. It just ... makes difficulties." She gave Ember a wan smile. "Thank you for sending me to a healer. The venom could have proved fatal. I've heard there have been many incidents in the prince's hallways. He cannot control his temper." Her hand flew up to her mouth, and she flung herself into a deep curtsey. "I apologise, my lady. All I meant was ..."

"Don't apologise. We all know what his temper is like." Shadows, snakes, smoke, and fear. If he won the tournament, if he became the Sword ...

She spent a quiet afternoon in her rooms, sitting on the window seat and gazing out into the grounds. The fairies that hovered around her windowsill hadn't returned and the eerie darkness of Cole's temper that influenced his side of the castle crawled under her door as a mist that clung to the ankles and made everything damp and clammy. When a heavy knock at the door came, she jumped.

A guard stood outside, with several others behind him. In his full-face helmet, she couldn't tell if he was one of those who had dragged her from the forest, and she eyed him with trepidation.

"His Highness summons you to the great hall at once," he said.

She slid off the window seat and twitched her skirts into place. "You stay here," she said to Mira. "I'll not have you come to harm again."

Mira was surprised but gave a curtsey, and the guards closed around Ember and took her away.

This time she was careful to keep an eye on the cracks and shadows in the halls, but apart from a swarm of black rats, red eyed and yellow fanged, chased off with several well-placed spear points, they made it to the hall without incident.

The doors opened, and the guards hustled Ember inside. It was the hall where she had first dined with Cole and the rest of the teams, although now there was no immense table down the middle, no glittering golden trees lining the walls, no music, no dancing.

Instead, three figures stood on a central round dais: Cole, the Adjudicator and Ashe. Fae clustered around the dais, and she recognised members of both teams, hushed and expectant. The jurors stood among them in silence, the red of their cloaks like scattered drops of blood.

As they brought her in, all turned to stare. Cole's expression of disgust was almost palpable, and the remaining members of his team viewed her with curled lips and muttered comments. Ashe's team, on the other hand, looked positively jubilant. She wished they didn't. They made it look as though she'd sabotaged Cole on purpose. Swirl didn't look angry though. He gave her a courteous nod, and she took heart from that.

The guards escorted her to a position below the dais, and she looked up at the three of them: Cole furious, Ashe typically blank-faced. Neither so much as glanced at her.

The Adjudicator showed a repellent smile filled with sharp, jagged teeth. He didn't look angry, merely amused, as if something new had finally surprised him. He eyed Ember and said, "You've thrown, as they say, a spanner in the works." He raised his voice. "Does anyone here know what a spanner is?"

Apparently, no one did.

The Adjudicator continued, "Cole's team cannot compete in the third game, which makes the winner, by default, Ashe."

Cole's face darkened, and he clenched his fists. The Adjudicator laughed, a thin, reedy, mirthless laugh that sent shivers up Ember's back. "Oh, stop, Cole. Your chances at best were fifty-fifty."

"The castle intervened! Surely an exception can be made! Lissa wasn't the only water sprite in the kingdom. Replace her and give me a chance!"

The Adjudicator shrugged. "The rules are clear. Once the teams are announced, no fae can replace a teammate, and the teams must be evenly matched. You signed the contract. You assumed the responsibility of heir when Serafina was ... well. Let's not talk about that. It seems we have our winner."

Ashe was frowning, not at all as pleased as Ember had thought he would be. His team wasn't so reticent. They broke into loud cheers and hugged one another.

"Wait!" Cole cried over the clamour. "This isn't right, this isn't fair." He pointed at Ashe. "He should kill one of his teammates, so we're even."

Ashe gave him an incredulous stare. "I don't think so."

"Without a winner, the Earth is on the tipping point again." The Adjudicator addressed Ember and there was glee in his voice. "You should see it! Wildfires are out of control across three continents. Heat waves are killing more people than ever! Our worlds are too close. Without a Sword, your world will burn."

"I don't care about that!" shrieked Cole. "It's not fair. This can't be the end. This can't be ..."

He stopped, frowning in thought, and then his expression cleared. "No fae can replace a teammate," he said, echoing the Adjudicator's words.

The Adjudicator waited; his eyebrows raised. "And?"

Cole pointed a finger at Ember. "But she can."

CHAPTER 37

T he hall fell silent. The Adjudicator let out a high-pitched
screech that echoed around the room, a hideous approximation
of a laugh that sounded more like a cry of pain.

Ember jerked her head back, a wave of disorientation threatening to
tip her sideways. "You cannot be serious." Her voice was a mere croak,
and her hands shook. She could smell her own fear, sharp and rank.

"You made the mess," Cole snapped. "You clean it up."

The Adjudicator clapped his wrinkled hands together in delight.
His red eyes flicked from Cole to Ashe to Ember, and she shrank from
his piercing gaze.

"It would fit the rules," he mused. "And rules are everything."

He turned to Ashe, who shrugged. "I have no objection."

One of the Winged Eagles on Ashe's team cried out, "No!" but was
hushed by those nearby.

Ashe looked over at them and lifted his chin. His voice was reso-
nant, defiant. "I don't want to win my kingdom by default. I don't
want my people questioning whether I have the divine right to rule."

Cole scowled. "You might not win, you know."

"With her?" Ashe gave a snort of disbelief. His supporters broke into helpless laughter, and even the Adjudicator smiled.

Ember dropped her gaze to the floor, resentment flooding her. He didn't have to be so unkind, she thought. He hadn't even so much as glanced at her since she'd walked into the room. She'd thought he was a friend, a distant, difficult friend, to be sure, but now it seemed he wasn't anything, just like everyone else.

"My magic will run through her veins!" shouted Cole, and a hush fell over the room. "My power will take this kingdom."

"Then so it shall be," said the Adjudicator. He pointed at Ember, and she felt it as though he had stroked a withered finger down her cheek. "You, human, shall take the sprite's role in the third game."

Ember's hand fluttered to her chest, her fingers cold. Her ears were ringing, the exclamations of the fae in the hall echoing and faint.

"Wait," she said. "Please ..."

Nobody listened. The Adjudicator stepped down from the dais, the jurors immediately surrounding him to escort him from the Hall. Ashe's and Cole's guards swarmed them both, and they too were hustled away to doors on the opposite sides of the hall. Ashe's team went next, giving Ember unfriendly glances, except for one sprite who said, "Thanks for getting rid of that stuck-up bitch for us," and the rest of the team snickered.

A guard grasped Ember's elbow to haul her off, but a voice stopped him.

"Let her go, you damn fool." Swirl was at her side, shoving the guard aside with his shoulder. "She's on the team now. Show her some respect." The guard bowed and stood aside. Swirl's brown eyes were kind. "You'd better come with me, girl."

The gentleness in his voice almost undid her, and she went with him without question, her feet tripping uncertainly on the floor-boards, her gut twisting with nausea.

The centaur's rooms looked more like a stable than a bedroom proper, with great feed bins and a pile of straw, but there was still an enormous bed covered with a luxurious velvet throw, and a lounging area with chairs and a low table for two-legged guests.

A healer was called, and Swirl bade him to massage her to release muscle tension. While the centaur busied himself looking through various papers, the healer stripped her and then treated her to a long, delicious massage that soothed and calmed her body. Her panic and distress soon faded to a resigned acceptance. She was only on the team to make up the numbers. They weren't expecting miracles from her. And if she were to be killed in the game, so be it. That might give Ashe the advantage he would need to win. If her death might help the kingdom and all the fae who lived there—for she couldn't see how Cole's rule would be anything other than a disaster—then that would be a fair price to pay.

When he was done, the healer helped her dress and then Swirl beckoned her to the lounge area. He spread a wide sheet of parchment on the table. "The Junction waterway."

It was a beautifully drawn map of the area just outside the castle walls, glamoured to make it look as realistic as a three-dimensional model, with tiny birds flying over the forests and little cows grazing in the fields.

Swirl pointed out a river that cut into two routes, each side flowing around an island forest before rejoining on the other side. "The game starts here," tapping one side of the river. "You swim along here ..." he broke off and looked up at her in alarm. "You can swim, can't you?"

She nodded, and Swirl laughed. "Well, that's good. Otherwise, it would be the shortest game in history. You swim along here and then you can choose left or right. Each way has its own dangers, not to mention the other team. They're experienced and armed. Your best hope is to stick with your team and hope they won't try to take revenge for Lissa's death. You'll get a dagger and a spear."

To her shame, she thought she might burst into tears. "I'm so sorry about all this."

Swirl patted her shoulder with a heavy hand. "None of this is your fault. You're the innocent. Lissa got what was coming. And no matter who wins, the little people, us, we'll just carry on, living our lives, trying to stay out of their way. The real danger will come once the Sword is crowned. I hear the Seeds are discontent. They want to extend their territories."

His words washed over her, but she was too busy studying the map to pay him much mind. The only thing that mattered to her right now was getting through the game. "Would you choose left, or right?"

"Me? Neither. I hate the water. But don't worry too much. When His Highness fills you with his power, you won't feel like you anymore. You'll be ... *better*. Your senses will be heightened, your reactions quicker, stronger."

"What does it feel like?"

"As though you have molten lightning running through your veins."

He called for two guards to escort her back to her rooms and gave her a warm hug as she left, which gave her comfort.

It surprised her to find that the hallways were clear. There were no unexpected skittering sounds, no gnashing of teeth from the shadows, and she wondered if Cole's temper had finally dissipated or if this was a courtesy extended only to members of his team.

She opened the door of her bedchamber, expecting Mira to be alone, but there was Cole pacing back and forth, and Mira herself standing with her forehead pressed to the wall, her wings wrapped around her as though to cocoon her from harm.

"Finally," he said, disagreeably. "I hope you know I'm very displeased."

Ember wasn't sure what to say. One wrong word could spark another tantrum, and she didn't have the energy to deal with that, so she said nothing.

"Did Swirl show you the course?"

She nodded. Cole came to her and took her hands. "Listen, my darling. You have been very naughty, but I understand most of it wasn't your fault. Lissa was always volatile. Many disliked her. I wasn't aware that the castle disliked her, too. Fancy choosing a human over ..." he broke off and took a deep breath. "But if you win this, if *we* win this, you will be rewarded, I promise."

"And if I lose?"

"You'll be dead," he told her. "And then it won't matter."

He ran a hand down her cheek and she, so pathetically grateful for a kind touch that she leaned into him and closed her eyes. He brushed her lips with the lightest of caresses. "Sleep, my dear. The Adjudicator has announced the game is to be brought forward. We compete tomorrow."

He left then, and Ember only just managed to stagger to her bed before her knees gave out. Mira was with her in seconds, plumping the pillows and smoothing the covers. She took out a lilac sleeping rose from her pocket, and Ember gratefully inhaled the intoxicating fragrance. She fell back against the pillows and didn't wake until morning.

CHAPTER 38

E mber kept her head down as the guards escorted her past the spectators and to the pavilion. There was no wine and a soft cushion for her this time, no little treats and music, no gossip and laughter filling the air. The fae supporting Cole were done with frivolity, and the weight of their disapproval was almost tangible. This game was too important.

In stark contrast, Ashe's team on the other side of the river were enjoying themselves as much as ever. Music and laughter drifted on the breeze, and sparkles streaked high above the dark pavilion, like fireworks. Tiny boats, festooned with flowers, and only large enough for two, were sailing merrily back and forth, although the fae aboard were careful not to drift over the midway point into Cole's territory.

She passed the other water sprites on her team, all aloof creatures, so devastated at losing their captain and teammate Lissa that they could barely look at her, let alone speak to her. She had the idea that they thought they could win just as well as without her, and they left her strictly alone.

The guards escorted her to the throne where Cole waited, his bearing ramrod straight, the familiar cloud around him pulsing with energy, crackling, and hissing. The events of the day before seemed to have galvanised him. He was in fighting form, at the peak of his abilities, and he had conjured a power that was awe-inspiring.

The air was cool around her, and she, clad in a sleek white swimsuit that looked as if sewn from fish-scales, shivered as little bumps stood up on her arms. But the closer she drew to Cole, the warmer the air became until she stood bathed in heat, not that of a comforting fireplace on a chilly winter's day, but as though she were about to be burned.

Cole made a sharp gesture, and she gasped in shock, hands fluttering up to her neck to find gaping wounds. He had slashed her across the throat. She tore her fingers away, expecting to see blood, but there was nothing, and after the initial cutting sensation, she felt absolutely no pain at all.

"Gills," said Cole, watching her tentatively exploring her throat. "You'll be underwater a time. Your team will support you. Stay close."

Ember was fairly sure they'd do no such thing. If the scylla in the water didn't kill her, she could bet that one of her teammates might, just to avenge Lissa. She was on her own.

He closed his eyes, which she took for dismissal, and the guards took her away.

She and her team of water sprites marched out onto the riverbank and waited for the gong, stretching, limbering up legs and arms. Someone thrust a dagger into the belt at her side, and Swirl, shouldering aside the fae clustered all around, brought her a light spear, tipped with a deadly glittering point.

He strapped it into a holster at her back, although how she would use it when she was in the water, she had no idea.

The gong sounded, a thundering crash that first silenced the watching fae, and then as the reverberations faded, they burst into cheers. Threads of white arced overhead, criss-crossing through the air and striking the water sprites in the chest, one by one. The fae gasped and moaned as Cole's power hit them, arching their backs, their faces contorted.

Last in line, Ember clenched her fists as a beam of white light fell toward her. She squeezed her eyes shut, waiting with trepidation for the agony and ecstasy of Cole's power flowing through her. Unlike the other beam, it hesitated just before it hit her, a hesitation that was long enough for her to crack an eye quizzically to see it poised, like a snake about to strike. In a rush, as though it had finally made up its mind, it dived into her, cleaving aside flesh, blood, muscle, bone, to strike at her heart.

And in that moment, she felt … nothing.

Not a damn thing.

Cole had no power over her. He might hurt her physically, but he didn't control her mind or her heart. The notion was thrilling. She arched her back and let out a cry that sounded like the others, but unlike the others, hers was a cry of triumph and release. She was free.

Almost.

As one with the others, she dived into the churning waters. Her team immediately banked left with the current, and she followed them. Ashe's team had gone right, against the flow, and she wondered why. Perhaps the ease of travelling with the water made for more danger ahead.

Tangles of weed carpeted the riverbed, and it was impossible to tell how deep the river was. The rush of the water was cool and sweet and there were a confused couple of moments when she automatically held her breath. Tentatively, she sucked in a gulp of water that fizzled through her gills, and then she was swimming properly, shooting through the water like a seal. Glee rose within her as the water both surrounded and infiltrated her. She *was* water. She could swim like this forever, she thought, wild and free, and —

A streak of fire whizzed past her leg, and she let out a yelp that was nothing but aggrieved bubbles. Two scylla swimming up from the watery jungle of plants below were attempting to cut her from off the main group. They swam on either side, trying to steer her toward the bank, and one aimed a green stick at her, a streak of fire shooting from its tip.

She ducked, and the fire shot harmlessly over her head. She swam faster, catching up with the water sprites in her team and gesturing wildly toward the danger. Only one turned; the others ignored her. The one who had taken heed of Ember's warning drew her dagger and slashed, spilling green scylla blood.

Ember drew her spear, and to her surprise, found it moved through the water with no drag at all. It acted as if it would in the open air. She thrust, skewering the remaining scylla in the throat, and it fell away. The water sprite gave her a congratulatory look, and they both swam on.

A yawning chasm showed black ahead, and as the group made to swim over it, a crowd of beings erupted from the depths, all flowing hair and sharp teeth and dark skin wrapped in rough shark leather. Two grabbed one of Ember's teammates and hauled him, kicking and thrashing, into the maw. Another slashed at a sprite, and blood erupted forth. The creature bit into the sprite's neck and chewed, the lifeless head falling sideways. The water was churning with limbs, weapons, and blood. It was hard to see. Ember felt a grab at her arm, and she blindly jabbed with her dagger. The creature clutched at the gaping wound, and another sprite swam in and finished her.

As the current pulled them relentlessly forward, the beings fell back, seemingly disinclined to leave the safety of the abyss.

The team was smaller now, and they swam on in a pack, Ember at the heart of them. She had proved herself, and there was strength in numbers.

The water churned ahead, a fizzing and bubbling, as the river joined that of the other side. The group moved toward the bank, to put as much distance as they could between theirs and Ashe's team, a wise course of action as the rivers converged and another group of five sprites swam into view.

Neither seemed inclined to engage the others in a fight, and it became a race. Ember pulled through the water as best she could, but even with the gills that Cole gifted her, she couldn't swim as swiftly as her teammates, and fell behind.

The water sprite she had earlier warned of the scyllas fell back with her, urging her on. Ember valiantly tried, but she was becoming weary, her arms and legs straining with effort.

Suddenly there was a wild agitation in the water ahead, a swirling froth of bubbles overcoming the swimmers. Through the maelstrom there came the gleam of silver scales, and the flick of an enormous tail. Immense fish with rows of pointed teeth were darting and diving amongst the sprites, tearing at flesh, gulping dismembered limbs whole. Blood clouded the water.

Ember and her teammate paused in horror and moved swiftly toward the bank, skirting the massacre. Another from Ashe's team had escaped the slaughter and was trailing in their wake, but she was swimming with one arm, the other broken and dangling.

With nothing impeding their way, Ember and the sprite swam on until they could see thick bands of gold streaming through the water, showing them the end. They rose to the surface, suffused in light.

Ember crawled up onto the bank. Her legs could hardly support her, and she lay there for a moment or two, until her single remaining teammate helped her to her feet. She could still hear the drumming of water in her ears, and it took her a moment to realise that the sound was cheering on all sides, cheering for her, cheering for the team, and cheering for Cole.

He emerged from the pavilion, a guard on either side to steady him. As always after a competition, his face was pale, and he was weak. But he had strength enough to push the guards aside and stand on his own, his face suffused with an unholy joy. "The Kingdom of Swords is mine!"

Ember cast a glance across the river, to where Ashe's supporters stood. They were clapping too, but it was automatic and half-hearted, and several were weeping. Some expected to die, others to be demoted from their free status to that of servants. Cole wasn't known for his mercy.

Cole spoke a few words to the water sprite next to her, who blushed coquettishly and made a graceful curtsey, and then he turned to Ember, taking her chilly hands in his. "Thank you, my darling. Thank you for this."

He kissed the back of one hand, and then the other, and she closed her eyes.

The Sword would be crowned, the wrong cousin chosen, and it was all her doing.

CHAPTER 39

A ll the fae of the castle would be at the crowning ceremony, with many more coming in from the surrounding countryside. The fae from the visiting kingdoms had made their departures as soon as they could, not wanting to be caught in a kingdom of Cole's making, all too aware of his elemental, capricious, and fickle nature.

The Seeds had left presents of precious medicines, inks, and intoxicants, all distilled from rare jungle flora. The Sands had likewise left gifts: gold dust that could be fashioned into statues with a single blown breath, and valuable panels of marble lace. The Skies and Stones however, had left without so much as a word, clearly demonstrating their disdain for the new ruler.

In her rooms, Ember was being made up and dressed. She had tried to escape the ceremonies, to avoid seeing the look of condemnation in Ashe's eyes, or the wild triumph in Cole's, but it was impossible. Everyone would want to see the human who had helped her lover become ruler. Everyone would want to see what Cole did with her next.

To regain some measure of control, she had refused to wear the elaborate gown Mira prepared, all ribbons and ruffles and glittering sequins, saying she had no wish to draw attention from His Highness, the Sword-in-waiting. Instead, she had asked for something simple. Mira had conceded, providing a simple sheath in midnight blue that left one shoulder exposed, and a slit that showed the length of her thigh. It was still elegant but gave Ember much more freedom of movement.

That Cole now ruled the kingdom was without doubt, as there wasn't so much as a single guard waiting to escort her to the great hall. Perhaps now that the other kingdoms were gone, she was deemed free from potential harm, but perhaps it was because she now belonged to the Sword, and no one would dare to attack her. There was no way she would accidentally run into Ashe in the forest or anywhere else, not when he was to be imprisoned in the pendant until Cole's death.

She and Mira moved through the hallways, newly decorated with bunting and fresh flowers. Fireworks sparkled through every window, glamoured to appear in the glass to be viewed only from within the castle. When they came to the stone corridors, the common areas where all might tread, most of the surrounding fae were laughing and chattering together, all dressed in their finest. But there were others, the supporters of Ashe, sombre and grim, their footsteps dragging.

The hall had been magically extended once again. The tree stood in the centre, flames burning brighter than she had ever seen them, while the pendant pulsated within the tree trunk, looking like a glowing heartbeat. The room was warm, but a translucent barrier arched over the top, an oily swirl of rainbow colours dripping down the sides, an enchanted shell to protect the fae from blazing heat.

On a dais, stood the Adjudicator, Cole, and Ashe; Cole with exultation dripping from every pore, Ashe with his head held high, as regal as though it were he who was being crowned.

The crowd was immense, and yet as she stood among them, quietly to one side with Mira, Ashe looked directly at her. Her lips parted, and she drew in a shaky breath. His eyes were eloquent, not with condemnation that she had helped his team to defeat, but as though he understood and forgave her. His searing gaze, the press of bodies around her and the tree itself, heating the room with its warmth despite the protective barrier, were making her head spin.

"I need a breath of fresh air," she told Mira, who was deep in animated conversation with the fae next to her.

"I'll come with you, my lady," Mira said.

"Oh no, we'll lose our places. I'll only be a minute," and then at Mira's protestations, "Don't be silly! No one will hurt me. I'm practically a celebrity."

She slipped back through the crowd to the doors. The guards stepped aside, and she moved into the cool of the outer corridor with relief.

It was the first time she'd been alone in a long, long time. She threw a quick smile to a group of fae hurrying to the hall lest they be late, and they smiled back, calling their congratulations. Celebrity indeed, she thought. A week ago, they would rather have spat on her than smile at her.

Slipping into a quiet alcove, she asked for a guide, and when the light appeared, she told it where she wanted to go.

Then she took off her slippers and started running.

She wasn't sure exactly where Cole's room was located. She had only ever been taken there by magic, but the guide didn't falter or appear to be lost. It just whizzed ahead of her, slowing down to let her catch up, and then speeding off again.

She held her skirt in one hand as she ran, thinking how much slower she would have been with a tonne of frilly fabric holding her back. Down a set of steps, through a long gallery lined with paintings, paintings that looked vaguely familiar, and she wondered if they'd been copied from famous Earthly works. She couldn't remember. Cole had stolen those memories and replaced them with poisoned kisses.

Finally, she came to a dark hallway ending with a heavy oak door. She took hold of the iron door handle and gently turned it. The guide shot away, and she entered the room, shutting the door behind her. The scent of Cole's room enveloped her, redolent of leather, sex, and spices. It made her want to gag.

In normal times, she supposed guards would have been standing at the door, swords drawn, but they, like every other fae, were in the hall to witness Cole taking the pendant from the flaming tree and hanging it around his neck.

Except ...

Ember put a hand in her pocket and slowly took out the pendant, laying it in her palm. The jewel was as orange as fire, but there lay a dark shadow within that turned and twisted, the old Blade that had been waiting to be replaced by the new.

Only now he was going to have to do his job just a little while longer.

It had been during the second game, the game of Air, when she had found herself alone as everyone surged outside to view the Winged Eagles being struck by white lightning, and then flying off to retrieve their golden apples. The white fog of Cole's power had hidden the guards from her view and she from theirs, and it was the work of a moment to wield the brush she had concealed in her pocket, and glamour herself invisible. Once away from the pavilion, she had drawn a simple pair of wings and flown back to the castle and to the hall of the flaming tree, trusting that the crowds caught up in the excitement of the game would conceal her absence.

She had been in such a hurry she hadn't even thought about what would happen if she were wrong. Would the tree burn her alive, as it had the Seeds fae on the night of the masquerade? It had come down to that—a decision between life and death, and she didn't care which, as long as she could make that choice herself, to have control over her destiny.

As she'd moved closer to the tree, the flaming leaves and branches had blazed higher. But it was just a gentle radiating heat that warmed and soothed her. She'd simply walked to the tree, taken the pendant down, and glamoured a new one to take its place.

She'd dithered then, wondering if she should just use it then and there, but she'd decided against it. She wanted Ashe to have the pendant. Ashe would be the best choice as ruler. He was considered, thoughtful, just. If he won the games, he would send her back, she was sure of it. But if Cole won ... she couldn't let him have it, she couldn't.

So, she'd hidden it under the mass of white roses at her windowsill, and flown back to the game, just in time to see Broude fall, and Cole's team achieve victory. No one had missed her. No one had asked where she was except Mira. She would have tried to leave after the third game, but she was constantly under surveillance, and the only place she was certain Cole would be was on the dais at the ceremony. Now was her last chance, her only chance.

She moved to the mirror and said, "Please show me where I came from."

She'd only ever seen the mirror showing the Earth cityscapes that Cole admired so much. This one was no different, a night in a distant place, with tall lighted structures and a building shaped like a needle, rising higher than the rest. The glass turned a smoky grey, and the city faded. As though she was on the back of a winged horse looking down between the clouds, she saw a street below her, the houses new, gardens carefully tended. She didn't recognise it. It frightened her.

The pendant twitched in her hand as though it knew she was about to call on it, and she gathered her strength and dropped the chain around her neck. The pendant fell against her breastbone.

The ground gave a mighty wrench, flinging her to the ground. Timbers split above her, the stone floors underfoot groaned, and there appeared a crack in the wall as though a tremendous axe had wrought it apart, biting in deep. She screamed, hands covering her head lest the ceiling fell in. And then came a voice, a terrible, hysterical cry resonating throughout the castle ...

"Where is she?!"

Ember struggled to her feet, but the ground pitched as though she were standing on the deck of a ship, and she had to grab the post of Cole's bed for support. For an instant, the mirror flashed and showed her reflection, wide eyed and dishevelled, the pendant glowing softly against her skin. There came another unearthly shriek, and she realised Cole knew. He had seen her through the mirror. He knew she was in his room and what she was about to do.

"Show me where I come from!" she screamed at the mirror, and the power of the pendant forced it to show the street, the inconsequential street that meant everything. "Tana, please, my Blade, rip the veil between our worlds and send me home."

The mirror cracked. Light poured from within, illuminating Ember with sunshine from another place, throwing the forever twilight room into light.

The door crashed open and rebounded against the wall. Cole stood in the doorway, no longer the golden-haired, handsome fae for whom she had fallen, but a twisted, unearthly representation of the worst of humanity: hate, rage, terror, horror, and death. And behind him, a darker shadow in black, giving her courage.

In two strides, Cole was across the room. He reached for her with fingers like claws, but the power of her Blade protected her, and he shrieked and jerked his hands back, his skin already raw red and blistered from the protective shield shimmering around her.

The mirrored glass split further apart. She took one last look at Cole, twisted with rage and pain, and at Ashe, tall, calm, resolute. And then she stepped forward, into the crack, into the veil between her world and theirs.

Cole's shrieks cut off as soon as she had stepped through. A shimmering empty stretch of nothingness surrounded her, that stretched on and on and on.

"Tana." Her voice was muffled, strange and insubstantial, the sound of a soap bubble popping in silence. "Let them not follow me."

The veil became thicker, more substantial, a fog that became like porridge, and she fought to move, her arms and legs trapped by viscosity, the sludge creeping up her torso, crushing her ribs. It felt as though her heart was struggling to pump her lifeblood, and she struggled for breath, her lungs constricted. The veil was no longer a thick white cloud, but shades of mottled grey, and she understood the colour was changing because of her, and if she didn't get out, she would die.

She forced a leg forward, as though she were wading through thick mud, dragging the other forward. Another step. And then ...

She fell out of the veil and onto a road, a backpack landing next to her. At once, a stream of memories came blasting into her mind and she recoiled, a hand to her head, crying out with the pain of remembering. Sunshine blazed through her closed eyelids, and she sucked in a shaky breath and then another.

There came a roar, a familiar throaty roar of a Mustang, and a car she knew drove slowly past the cul-de-sac, the sound of the engine fading into the distance.

She was back. She was back.

Epilogue

People crowded the gallery, laughing, chatting, and discussing the works on display. Jean-clad student servers with trays of sparkling wine wandered throughout, offering glasses left and right.

Ember stood to one side, a solemn figure in black pants and a black shirt, her uniform of choice now. Nobody had ever seen her wear any other colour, and it had become her signature look.

Behind her hung a huge painting of a gothic castle wreathed in mist. The cloudy haze held suggestions of fantastical creatures crouching in the gloom, but the more one looked, the more one couldn't be sure. The figures and faces were only visible if one wasn't looking directly at them, and more than one group had taken up position in front of it for a time, staring at it and then looking away, hoping to glimpse its secrets.

The painting was a standout piece amongst the others of her class, and she had already been offered three commissions and the chance to show her paintings at the gallery once she had enough for a solo exhibition. The evening was a triumph for Ember, and she accepted it gladly and with quiet dignity.

The gallery slowly emptied until only a few remained, including her art tutor, who was more than a little drunk and hugged Ember so tightly she thought her ribs might crack. "I'm so happy for you," she kept saying, dabbing at her eyes with a used serviette. "You're really going places, Ember. I've had the paper asking about you. They want to do a review."

Ember shook her head. "Oh no. I don't want that."

"But you need exposure. How else will you sell your paintings?"

Ember gave a tight smile and accepted another hug, assuring her tutor she'd think about it. She was on the other side of the country now. There was little chance Bruno would find her, and besides, it had been three years now.

She went to find her coat in the back room, shrugging it on with relief, for the night was getting chilly. The relentless heat of the last few years had cooled, and people were wondering if this was it, if climate change had finally stabilised. Scientists were cautiously optimistic, and governments were smugly congratulating themselves. There hadn't been an unusual weather event in months.

Ember emerged from the back room and made to leave, pausing at the door as she saw someone new standing in front of her painting, considering it closely. She looked around for the curator or her tutor, wondering if they could take over the spiel about the work. She was exhausted. The strain and the excitement of the last few days needed to be soaked away in a hot bath.

But she couldn't see either of them, and so she approached the viewer with a rehearsed smile on her face, wondering which of her stock phrases to begin with. "Do you like it?" "I'm sorry, it's been sold," or, "Hello, I'm the artist."

But as he turned to face her, she froze, her hand automatically covering the orange pendant that hung around her neck, the pendant that she never took off, not ever.

His dark eyes seared her, the mouth as deliciously grim as she remembered, and his tone was biting as he said, "Hello, Ember. I think we need to talk."

TO BE CONTINUED ...

And Finally ...

Thank you for reading the first full length book set in the fairytale world of Esha! Please consider giving it a rating or review on your favourite book platform. For more info on all things Esha, visit my website at www.tabithaday.com/

Ember's adventure continues in
"Betrayal of the Sword"
Chronicles of Esha 2

BOOKS BY TABITHA DAY

The Chronicles of Esha Series

Capture of the Blade

Crowning of the Sword

Betrayal of the Sword

Destiny of the Sword

Summoning Skies

Skies of Blood